ALONE *With* YOU

— STORIES —

Marisa Silver

Simon & Schuster

New York London Toronto Sydney

Simon & Schuster
1230 Avenue of the Americas
New York, NY 10020

"Temporary," "The Visitor," and "Night Train to Frankfurt" originally appeared in *The New Yorker.*

"Leap" originally appeared in *Ecotone.*

"Three Girls" originally appeared in *Electric Literature.*

"Alone With You" originally appeared in *Five Chapters.*

First Simon & Schuster hardcover edition April 2010

SIMON & SCHUSTER and colophon are registered trademarks of Simon & Schuster, Inc.

For information about special discounts for bulk purchases, please contact Simon & Schuster Special Sales at 1-866-506-1949 or business@simonandschuster.com.

The Simon & Schuster Speakers Bureau can bring authors to your live event. For more information or to book an event contact the Simon & Schuster Speakers Bureau at 1-866-248-3049 or visit our website at www.simonspeakers.com.

Designed by Akasha Archer

Manufactured in the United States of America

10 9 8 7 6 5 4 3 2 1

Library of Congress Cataloging-in-Publication Data
Silver, Marisa.
    Alone with you : stories / Marisa Silver.
      p. cm.
    1. Families—Fiction.   2. Short stories, American—21st century.   I. Title.
PS3619.I55A78   2010
813'.54—dc22   2009051114

ISBN 978-1-4165-9029-3
ISBN 978-1-4165-9386-7 (ebook)

For my mother and my sisters

Contents

....

Temporary

. . . .

Vivian and Shelly lived in downtown Los Angeles, in an industrial space that belonged, nominally, to a ribbon factory whose warehouse was attached. Shelly discovered it one night when the band she belonged to had played at an impromptu concert there. When the evening was over and everyone had cleared out, Shelly and a man she'd met that evening stayed on. The man left soon afterward, but Shelly did not. She worked out an arrangement with the owner of the ribbon factory: the rent would be paid in cash, and if Shelly was discovered by the housing authorities, the owner would claim that she was a squatter.

Vivian met Shelly at the temp agency where they both applied for work. She had just finished two years of community college in Oklahoma and moved to L.A. Shelly offered her a small room in return for half the rent. She couldn't guarantee that they wouldn't be thrown out in a week or a month, but it was cheaper than the motel where Vivian had been staying, where she had to get out of bed two or three times a night to check the lock on the door whenever a drunken couple pinballing past caused it to rattle in a way that unnerved her. At Shelly's place, the thumps and grinds of machinery could be heard through the walls, but only during the day. In addition to Vivian's room, there was a doorless bathroom and a large open space. A rolling garage door served as the only window. You pulled on a chain and by some miracle of simple machinery the metal door ratcheted open with a satisfying flourish that appealed to Shelly's sense of drama.

Vivian had never met a girl like Shelly, who left her money lying around on tables and liked to throw blindfold dinner parties. Vivian had to learn not to compliment Shelly's clothes or jewelry because Shelly had a habit of taking off whatever it was that Vivian liked and giving it to her. Vivian also learned to be blasé about coming out of her room in the morning to discover Shelly sleeping with a man they had met the evening before—or a woman. Vivian felt a little thrill at being able to carry off such sophisticated nonchalance, and she admired the way Shelly slithered through her days and nights, shedding the most outrageous experiences as if they were simply the air she passed through. Shelly had negligible professional skills and wavering incentive, and only Vivian managed to get a temp placement—doing clerical work at an adoption agency. Still, Shelly managed to come home with bags full of mangoes and coconuts, and sometimes they drank margaritas and grilled steak on the loading dock outside the garage door, using Vivian's George Foreman. Shelly's last name was vaguely familiar to Vivian, as if she had seen it on packages at the grocery store, or maybe on television ads for insurance.

But she didn't ask, because she didn't want to appear ignorant, and because her parents had taught her that it was impolite to talk about money.

At the adoption agency, Vivian was put to work at a computer in a small, windowless room where office supplies were kept; the walls were lined with bales of toilet paper and paper towels, industrial-sized bags of coffee and nondairy creamer. Vivian's job was to transcribe the interviews recorded with prospective parents. These interviews were poorly taped, and Vivian spent her days winding the tape recorder back and forth in order to see if a husband had said that he loved children or loathed them, or if a wife had called herself infertile or infantile. Vivian herself was adopted—this was the single piece of information that had gotten her the job, as she typed only sixty words a minute and didn't know how to make a spreadsheet. Her adoptive parents were nice people. Until the recent recession put him out of business, her father had run a small jewelry store in a mall that catered mostly to young couples buying engagement rings and girls celebrating their *quinceañeras*. Her mother had worked as a secretary in a doctor's office. They were older than most parents and had required little of Vivian when she was growing up. They had always treated her with a kind of cautious respect that she didn't see many other parents accord their children. By the time she was ten, her father was sixty. At back-to-school nights, her parents stood by themselves while the younger parents exerted a kind of hysterical energy toward one another. "Oh, you're Alison's mother!" they'd say, as though Alison, with her accomplishments, bestowed a reflected glory on the parents who'd made her. No one came up to Vivian's parents to remark on Vivian, but this was understandable. Vivian was a "below-the-radar kind of girl," as her adviser had written on one midterm evaluation. This wasn't necessarily a bad thing, the adviser had added; not everyone could be a leader.

When Vivian was fourteen, her mother became sick and was on the verge of death. In her mother's hospital room, Vivian's parents told her that she was adopted. As it turned out, her mother made a miraculous recovery, but the cat was already out of the bag. The information didn't have much of an effect on Vivian. She lay in bed trying to feel different, now that she knew that her parents weren't her real parents, but she didn't feel different. The words *father* and *mother* were inextricably bound to the man and woman in the room down the hall, to her mother's Je Reviens perfume and her father's top dresser drawer filled with collar stays and golf tees. She was not imaginative enough to associate any other meaning with the words. She watched a television news show about a famous singer whose daughter had tracked her down after forty years. The famous singer seemed happy to have been found, and the two sat with their arms around each other and took long walks on the bluffs above the ocean, hand in hand. The women's intimacy made Vivian uncomfortable. Her own mother's kisses were dry, soft things, her hugs unassertive and prudent, as if she didn't want to cause Vivian any harm. There was a moment during the show when the two women looked at each other as if to say, "Now what?" and Vivian had the sense that the mother had some misgivings about being found, that having given up a child had become part of her personal mythology, her idea of herself. Now, faced with the real person, she had lost some of the romance of her story. Driving across the desert on her way to Los Angeles, Vivian had seen a billboard announcing that this same singer, who had been very popular in the seventies, would be performing five nights at a casino on an Indian reservation. This strengthened Vivian's decision not to explore her own adoption. You didn't always want to know everything.

Sometimes, when Vivian finished transcribing an interview at the adoption agency she would add a note to the bottom of the document offering her opinion of the interviewed couple. No one asked for her advice, but she felt compelled to give it since a life was at stake. Mostly she felt the couples should be allowed to adopt, because whatever flaws they had were no worse than the flaws of people who could have children effortlessly, even thoughtlessly, and she knew that children could survive almost anything. In one case, though, she felt strongly that the husband was unkind to the wife, and she noted this at the bottom of her transcript. She could not explain how she knew this, never having seen the couple. But the woman sounded frightened in a way that set her apart from the other women who were simply nervous during their interviews. She paused before each answer, as if waiting for the man's permission to speak, and at the end of her answers she always added, "Right, Paul?" The woman who ran the agency reprimanded Vivian for this insight and reminded her that her job was a temporary one. But Vivian kept track and she knew that the couple had not yet been matched with a child.

Shelly gave up looking for work. She said that she had too many projects of her own to concentrate on, and besides, she just wasn't "the office type." This statement seemed slightly insulting to Vivian, who clearly *was* the office type, but she could not discount Shelly's generosity—the way she paid when they went out to dinner or brought home expensive wine for them to share—and Shelly's rejection of such commonplace concerns as making a living seemed exotic to Vivian. Shelly spent most of her mornings wandering around their living space in a loosely tied mint-green kimono, her small, freckled breasts winking out from the material as she moved. For a time she took up painting and made large canvases on which she drew crude images of her face struck through with angry slashes of color. She organized a viewing of her work and a hundred strangers showed up at their home. Vivian wore one of Shelly's beaded dresses and Shelly wore body paint. The guests ate the food that Vivian and Shelly had prepared and refrained from buying anything. Shelly didn't seem to mind. After a few months the canvases disappeared, though it was unclear to Vivian whether someone had finally bought them or if Shelly had just thrown them into the Dumpster behind the ribbon warehouse to be carted away along with the giant spools of badly dyed grosgrain.

By this time Shelly had become involved with a man named Toby, who stood on corners in Silver Lake and Echo Park handing out pamphlets about the Socialist Workers Party. He was a quiet man who wore thick-framed glasses and collared shirts, which he tucked into his jeans. When he spoke to people he listened carefully as if they were giving him directions. He had gone to a very good college back East, and when he talked fervently about his political beliefs, Vivian admired his seriousness and his self-restraint, and the prominent tendons of his forearms. Shelly grunted a lot while having sex on the pullout, and in the mornings Toby left quickly, a ream of freshly printed flyers stuffed under his arm.

*   *   *

The couple whom Vivian had considered unsuitable for adoption had come back for a second interview. When Vivian turned on the tape recorder, the sound of the man's voice was so vivid that she looked over her shoulder thinking he was behind her. Instead of starting to type she pressed the headphones tightly to her ears and just listened to what was being said.

"Maybe we didn't make the right impression," the man said.

There was a pause, and then the wife said, "We have a lot of love to give. Right, Paul?"

"But that's what everybody says, of course," the man said. Vivian could hear the tension in his voice. He must have stood up at that point because as he continued his voice grew distant and full of air. "You must hear stupid, obvious things like that every day," he said. " 'We have a lot of love to give.' It's probably meaningless to you. But what else can we say? We want a child. We have enough money to offer a child a good life, all the advantages. We're decent people with decent values. But it feels like we're paying the price for some biological glitch we have no control over."

The director of the agency assured them that they had done well in the interview process, but that it was her job to match the right children with the right parents and this effort could take time.

"Some people don't test well," the man said. "Is that it?" His voice was louder, as if he were seated again.

The director told them that it wasn't a test.

"Sure it is," the man said. "Everything is a test."

When the interview was over Vivian sat listening to the sound of empty tape winding through the recorder. She rewound it and listened to the entire interview again. *Some people don't test well*. The way he said it made it sound like a kind of attack. It was as if he could open up the director's head, peer into her brain, and see all her prejudices and value judgments. When he talked about the "stupid, obvious thing" his wife had said, Vivian imagined the woman looking at her lap, embarrassed that the compromises of her marriage were being exposed to a stranger, and that it was she who would be considered weak for accepting these insults, rather than her husband for hurling them.

Vivian rewound the interview once again and began to input it into the computer. The words were familiar to her now and she tried to visualize the couple. She saw the man with dark, neatly cropped hair, muscular from hours at a gym. He was the kind of man who, when he was inside, wore his sunglasses on the back of his head like a pair of upside-down eyes. She imagined the woman as delicate and fair, clasping her hands as if they were wayward children who might break something if she let them go. She was beautiful, but rusted, as if her beauty had been abandoned, exposed to the elements. Vivian knew that she could be completely wrong about the couple. They might be fat. They might be Chinese. They might be the warmest people in the world who would lavish on their adopted child the sort of palpable love advertised in greeting cards or on the collars of stuffed puppies. How could anyone know what kind of love another person had to give?

When Vivian got home that night, Toby was there alone. He sat at the table reading a book, his back straight, his head bent as if in prayer.

"She went to a thing at a club," he said.

"You didn't want to go?"

"I guess I'm not a club person."

"Whatever that is," she said.

He looked up and smiled, which embarrassed her because she knew that they were both making fun of Shelly and in doing so forming a secret bond. Why wasn't Toby at his own house? Maybe Shelly had left him at hers the way she left hundred-dollar bills lying around, evidence of her carelessness. Shelly's sofa bed was open and unmade, red sheets spilling suggestively off the thin mattress. Vivian got a yogurt out of the refrigerator and a filigreed spoon from the old Ball jar that held the set of antique silver utensils that had belonged to Shelly's grandmother, and went to her room. She ate her yogurt but felt too awkward to go back out and throw the empty cup into the garbage so she left it on the floor by her mattress where it toppled over under the weight of the spoon. She tried to read a book but she couldn't concentrate knowing that Toby was in the other room, reading his book. She had to go to the bathroom. Somehow, when Shelly was home with Toby, using the doorless bathroom wasn't such a problem. But she couldn't imagine using it now. The more she thought about it, however, the more she needed to. She decided not to make eye contact with Toby as she crossed the main room. If she pretended that he wasn't there, maybe he would pretend that she wasn't there either. In the bathroom she peed quickly with her eyes closed as if he were the one who didn't want to be seen. The toilet made a grating mechanical sound when flushed, and the water pipes of the sink let out their customary screeching complaints, bedeviling Vivian's attempts at invisibility. After she'd dried her hands, she turned toward the doorway, and there he was.

"Sorry," he said. "I didn't hear you."

"You didn't hear me?"

"I guess I was into my book."

"What are you reading?"

"*Pnin,*" he said.

"Is it good?"

He glanced past her into the bathroom. "You finished in here?"

"Oh," she said, realizing that she was blocking the way.

She walked quickly back to her room, but not fast enough to avoid hearing his relieved groan and the hard stream as his piss hit the toilet bowl.

She took the empty yogurt cup and spoon to the kitchen area. He walked out of the bathroom, adjusting his jeans.

"Do you think you make a difference?" she said.

"What?"

"With your flyers. I mean, is anybody interested?"

"You're not, I guess."

"Do you really think people change their minds?"

"People change their minds all the time. I think I want a hamburger, but I order a pizza."

"That's a ridiculous comparison."

"Not really. That's how we progress as a culture. We change our minds and, little by little, we become something else."

"We become a more pizza-oriented culture," she said.

He smiled. He didn't seem offended.

"It's just, if someone walked up to me on the street and started talking about communism or socialism, I wouldn't stop to have a conversation."

He shrugged. "I'm not going to change your mind, then," he said.

The way he said this made her feel dismissed. She wanted to correct him. She wanted to be able to change her mind, wanted *him* to change her mind. Although he seemed to have convictions, he had the same careless quality as Shelly, a confidence that allowed them both to ride along above the dismal concerns of everyone else. Why did she care so much? Her care felt like a disfigurement, something that made it necessary for people like Shelly and Toby to distance themselves from her. Her care felt like something that would drag down the progress of human development. It made her an awkward, embarrassing person who asked what book you were reading when all you wanted to do was go to the bathroom. She felt her face flush and she returned to her room. She changed into her nightclothes and got into bed and turned off the lamp, but she was too agitated to sleep.

When Vivian's mother was sick, she'd stayed in the hospital for months at a time, and Vivian and her father learned how to get along in the house without her. Vivian cooked breakfast and dinner, and her father did the grocery shopping on his way home from the jewelry store. After dinner he would wash the dishes and Vivian would clean the table and the counters. They saw her mother every evening during visiting hours. Sometimes if her mother were very sick, Vivian wasn't allowed in the room, and she would sit in the waiting area until her father came out. He'd always say something cheerful, like "The doctor feels confident," or "She had a good day," and

Vivian would respond in kind, knowing he needed her to play along. Once back home, her father would turn on the television. He kept it on all night to avoid the new silence in the house.

One day Vivian decided that instead of going straight home from school she would take the bus to the mall and meet up with her father there. Maybe they could go out for dinner on their way to the hospital. After walking a block from the bus stop, she entered the dead weather of the mall. It was almost Easter, and a person dressed as a bunny hopped down the corridors, promoting a candy store by handing out chocolate eggs to children. Vivian rode the escalator to the second floor where her father's store was. Through the glass storefront, she saw her father come out from behind the counter to fasten a woman's necklace. The woman's neck was long and pale, and her dark hair was drawn to the side and over one shoulder to make way for the jewelry. When Vivian's father was finished with the clasp, he took the woman's hair and spread it carefully along her back, as if he were smoothing down a wrinkled dress. He rested his hands on the woman's shoulders while she admired herself in a handheld mirror. Vivian's throat went dry. She left the mall and took the bus home. She never asked her father about what she had seen. She knew that if she did, her life would split open and she would slip through the crack.

In a few months, Vivian's mother's recovery was certain, and she came home. She was weak for a time, resting in bed most of the day, but little by little she began to take up her household chores again, cooking and cleaning, although she never went back to work. One night, when Vivian and her parents were seated at the table about to eat their dinner, her father started crying. Vivian had never seen her father cry and it frightened her. He was just so happy, he said, shaking his head at the folly of his emotion. Vivian's mother sat in her chair and smiled shyly, like a girl watching a boy approach across a dance floor and realizing that he has singled her out from all the girls around her.

A knock on her door made Vivian realize that she had almost been asleep. The door opened a crack and Toby stood silhouetted against the light of the outer room.

"Shelly just called," he said. "She's not coming back to-night."

"Oh," Vivian said, sleepily, not quite understanding. But then she found herself moving over in bed and lifting the covers as an invitation. Toby stepped into the room, took off his clothes, and slid in beside her. His skin was warm, and when he moved on top of her Vivian felt the thin tautness of his body. She put her arms around his narrow shoulders as if he were a log floating in a river on which she could rest to catch her breath.

"Just for now," he whispered into her neck as he began to move faster on top of her. He was boyish in the way he announced his orgasm, and she felt protective of him as he rested, spent, in her arms. She wondered if she cared for him, if it mattered to her that tomorrow he would likely be gone for good, Shelly having obviously had enough of him. Was it possible to care and not to care at the very same moment, the way it was possible to be a husband and not, a parent and not?

*   *   *

The receptionist at the adoption agency went on maternity leave. Rather than hire another temp, the director decided that Vivian could manage her work while sitting at the front desk. She instructed Vivian on how to handle the prospective parents who came to the office to be interviewed. Vivian was to be polite and helpful in terms of offering water or coffee or directing them to the restrooms in the hallway, but not overly solicitous and definitely not optimistic in any way. Vivian was confused by this last directive; she was unsure how to be helpful without giving off an air of optimism. Most couples sat in the waiting room in silence, fearing, perhaps, that anything they said in front of the receptionist might be used against them.

One afternoon a man walked into the office. He was a small, compact man with what Vivian's mother would have called a "coif" of thick, shiny hair. He wore an elegant suit of a modern cut, the jacket purposefully small, the pants short enough to reveal his garishly printed socks. He stood in front of her desk, and a second before he opened his mouth to speak, Vivian realized who he was.

"Where's your wife?" she said, imagining that the man had forbidden his wife to come this time, that he had decided that her presence was what stood in the way of their getting a child.

"Excuse me?"

"Usually we see couples," Vivian said, covering for her blunder. She reminded herself to be polite and not optimistic. She didn't want to lose her job.

"I don't have an appointment," he said.

"She's doing an interview right now," Vivian said.

His face was anguished for a moment, as if he thought

that this other couple were, at that very moment, being granted the child he'd hoped would be his. Of course this was not the way it worked, but perhaps the man didn't know that.

"Is it okay if I wait?"

"I guess," Vivian said. "Do you want water? Or coffee?"

His face relaxed and opened up, and Vivian saw how great the barriers were between a person and his happiness, and how little it took to make him think they were small.

"I don't need anything," he said.

She tried to go back to her transcription, but she could not concentrate. She typed zzzzzz for an entire line, then ?????? for two more after that.

"My wife left me," he said.

She looked up. He was staring down at the checkerboard pattern on the linoleum floor as if it were a code he was trying to break.

"Oh," she said.

"Does she do single-parent adoptions?"

"I don't know," Vivian said. "I'm just a temp."

He nodded. His pants were so short, she could see his legs where his socks ended. The hair there was dark and smooth, as if combed.

The man stood up and walked over to the wicker shelf that held various books about adoption. He took down a paperback, flipped through it, put it back.

"Do you know what she looks for?" he said. "I mean, what type of people she accepts?"

"The stupid, obvious things," Vivian said. "People who have a lot of love to give." She was immediately ashamed of her small cruelty, but he did not seem to remember his own words.

He sat down again. "This is crazy. I don't even have an appointment."

Her job was temporary. The director had informed her that the receptionist, when she came back, would take on the work of transcribing the interviews along with her other duties. Vivian had proved that it could be done. Vivian had a feeling, too, that she would soon have to find a new living arrangement. Shelly had found out about the night with Toby and had said that she didn't care, but things felt different now.

"Why did your wife leave you?" Vivian asked.

The man looked at her, stricken. "I don't know," he said finally.

For some reason, she believed him. She was sure that he had all the information: perhaps his wife had had enough of his meanness; perhaps she had a lover; maybe she didn't like the fact that he was the kind of man who cared about fashion. Vivian believed that he understood the facts, but that, still, he didn't know.

Vivian's mother lived for another three years, until Vivian was seventeen and almost finished with high school. Toward the end, she began to lose her eyesight. The doctors said that this was a result of the tumor growing back—it was pressing on nerves. Surgery was out of the question; the tumor was clinging to the brain like a child to its mother, as if it didn't really believe that it was a separate thing in and of itself. This time, Vivian's mother told her that she was definitely going to die. She didn't want Vivian to think that because a miracle had taken place once it might again.

"And now we know," her mother said. "It wasn't a miracle after all."

Strangely, those last years were some of the happiest Vivian could remember. Her mother threw caution to the wind. They ate dinners of crackers and canned cheese if they felt like it. They watched movies until three in the morning, even on school nights. Her father's business was beginning to fail, and occasionally he brought home jewelry for Vivian and her mother. Vivian's mother would protest, but he rationalized these gifts, saying that he would have to lower the prices so drastically to make a sale that he might as well not sell the pieces at all.

"When I ordered this," he said, fastening a necklace around his wife's neck, "I imagined how it would look on you."

Vivian remembered him making the same gestures with the woman in the store that day, and it occurred to her that she might have misunderstood what she had seen. Her father might simply have been generous with a stranger. But she did not really believe this. As she watched her mother admire her new necklace in a mirror, Vivian realized that she would always have to choose what to believe, and that chances were, more often than not she would be wrong.

In the last month of her life, Vivian's mother took up smoking. She was completely blind by then. She had always wanted to smoke, she said. She thought that a woman with a cigarette looked elegant, even if it gave her cancer. Vivian bought a pack of Parliaments on her way home from school one afternoon. Her mother put a cigarette in her mouth and Vivian lit it for her with a long kitchen match. Her mother, too weak to sit up in bed, lay against her pillows and inhaled deeply. She coughed, and they laughed, but soon enough she got the hang of it, except that when she exhaled she did a funny thing: she blew out again and again, like a woman practicing for childbirth. She looked silly and not at all elegant, but Vivian didn't say anything because her mother seemed so happy. When her father came home that evening, he watched his wife enjoy her cigarette.

"What is that you're doing?" he said, as she exhaled.

"What?" she asked, her thin voice made even thinner by the stress of the smoke in her lungs.

"You look like a fish, sweetheart," he said, and he put his lips to her cheek and blew out puffs of air until she giggled. For a second, Vivian caught a glimpse of what her mother had looked like as a little girl.

"But I can't see. How do I know when all the smoke is gone?" Vivian's mother said, her voice coy, flirtatious.

"You don't have to worry about that," he said, brushing a strand of hair from her cheek. "It'll all come out in the end."

She smiled and took a drag on the cigarette. She let out a smooth trail of smoke. She kept her eyes closed as Vivian and her father watched the delicate curl of smoke dissolve and disappear, like sugar on the tongue.

Leap

. . . .

THE GIRLS WERE MANNING A LEMONADE STAND—A MEDIUM-SIZE
Dixie cup for fifty cents a cup, or a cup with a Hydrox cookie
for seventy-five. Sheila, her older sister Trudy, and Maggie
and Jeannie, ten-year-old twins who lived down the street, sat
on folding chairs behind the small card table the twins'
mother had loaned them. The backs of Sheila's thighs burned
from the heat trapped in the metal of her chair. She wore cu-
lottes, a combination of miniskirt and shorts. Sometimes she
thought of the outfit in the opposite way, as shorts mixed with
a miniskirt. But today it was the first version because Maggie
and Jeannie were both younger, and because, for once, Trudy
was not pressing down on Sheila's soul as if she were a
thumbtack.

    The man bought a glass of lemonade. He said, "I have a
problem. Maybe one of you girls can help me." He'd driven up

in his car and parked at a reckless angle to the curb, like the boys at school who refused to hang their coats on the hooks provided at the back of the classroom and let them fall to the floor in arrogant puddles. The man said his problem was that he needed to change his clothes. He gestured to Sheila with a wrinkled paper bag that she assumed was filled with his new outfit. He had a job interview, he said. A very important job interview.

"But I need someone to guard the door," he said.

"Why don't you change in your car?" Trudy said.

"That wouldn't be very private," the man said. "It might be embarrassing."

Sheila's body understood first, and then her brain followed, knowledge spreading out like a stain. She could tell by the penitent silence of the younger girls that they could tell something was wrong too. Still, no one screamed "Stranger, Danger!" the way they had been taught.

"Just around the corner," he said. "There's a little garden shed, but the door doesn't lock. Anyone could come in, and that would be embarrassing, wouldn't it?" The way he repeated the word made Sheila aware that embarrassment was somehow tangled up in pleasure.

"We can't help you," Trudy said. She was fourteen.

"Really?" he said. "Not even you?" He looked directly at Sheila.

Sheila was twelve. She wore a halter top and she liked the way the bumps of her new breasts felt against the nylon. The man's eyes searched her face, but she did not look away. She felt a curious ambivalence about his wrinkled paper bag, and the fact that he wanted to do something bad to her. What was "bad"? she wondered. How bad did a thing have to be before it was something you would never get over for the rest of your life? Two boys rode up on bikes. They asked how much for the cookies. Trudy said you couldn't buy cookies without lemonade, and the boys began to argue with her. When the boys didn't leave, the man got into his car and drove away. The little girls burst into giggles, and Trudy told the boys what had happened, exaggerating for effect. Sheila felt the way she did when she took a corner too quickly on her bike and an oncoming car swerved to avoid her; the sip of breath, the way she could see her life and her death at the very same moment. She put her arms across her chest to hold herself.

"What's wrong with you?" Trudy said.

"I'm cold."

"It's a hundred million degrees out here." The attention of the boys had unleashed Trudy's haughty condescension. She told everyone to pack up the stand. "Right away," she said, like their mother.

Sheila and Trudy walked home, carrying the plastic container half full of lemonade and an unopened bag of cookies. Sheila felt as if everyone were watching her—the lady kneeling by her flower bed, the kids across the street playing Chinese jump rope, even God. She was sure He was watching because something important had happened, some small shift that had a ripple effect. Suddenly, she felt beautiful and much older than she had been ten minutes earlier. She was certain of it. How silly Maggie and Jeannie looked to her, dragging the folding table and chairs across the lawn toward their house. How alive she felt, walking beside her older sister, the summer air touching her back like a warm hand.

"Don't tell," Trudy hissed, "or they'll never let us do anything ever again."

Sheila agreed to keep silent. She would never tell her parents that for the first time she had been taken seriously.

Sheila was thinking about that long-ago afternoon right before Patsy tried to kill herself. Sheila and Patsy were making their way through a development about a half hour from Sheila and Colin's house downtown. The residential area had burst into full-fledged existence the previous year. These shingle-roofed homes, meant to evoke a cleaner, less cumbersome version of the past, were so newly constructed that their pale decks had not yet weathered to an earthen brown. Sheila had chosen this inconvenient location because it was outside the city ordinance and she could walk Patsy without a leash, and because the development came complete with instantly mature and bucolic woods and a level, litigation-proof pathway. Sheila had undergone bypass surgery four months earlier, a shock at age thirty-seven, and although she was otherwise healthy and her doctors assured her that she could live a "normal life," she had grown wary. Assumptions that the earth would be there to meet her foot when she put it down, or that her body would remain upright without her expressly willing it to were no longer certain, and she found herself hesitating more than she used to, as though to give the world a chance to announce its true intentions. Sheila had been a springboard diver in high school, and occasionally she dreamed of diving, not of meeting the water, but of the seconds before, when she was suspended and gloriously weightless, when the possibility of disaster was unimaginable. When she woke, looking automatically at Colin, big and comfortably thick beside her in their bed, she wondered at the transparency of dreams.

The path hugged a ravine, and she and Patsy trotted to the edge of the embankment to look down at the stream below. The water moved sullenly; only the light coming through the trees and glancing off the stream's surface indicated the direction of the current. Sheila inhaled the moist, spoiled odor of the late fall and waited as it mixed with memory, creating a pleasing sorrow for irretrievable things. Patsy sniffed too, but only because that was her nature. Patsy was overweight— more barrel than dog—and Sheila had to suffer the condemnation of neighbors who would stop to inform her that her dog was fat and then list the medical conditions that would befall Patsy as a result of Sheila's negligence. A childless couple living in a neighborhood of families presented a troubling puzzle. People assumed Sheila must have been careless to have gotten into this situation, and that she needed their help.

Why did Patsy jump? There was no rustle in the bushes to alert the dog to a skunk or gopher, no distant bark to set her hair on end. There was no food below emitting its siren scent—Sheila knew this because she slid down the embankment on her backside to rescue Patsy and did not see a castoff hamburger wrapper or even an apple core.

Sheila carried the forty-pound, bristle-furred mutt to her car and drove to the veterinarian's office. While the doctor operated, Sheila sat in the waiting room, paging through limp pet magazines, inhaling the ammonia scent of urine mixed with disinfectant. A steady parade of sick animals and solicitous owners came in and out of the office. Sheila knew she should coo at the pets or inquire after their maladies but she was worried about Patsy. Two hours later, the vet appeared from the surgery and informed Sheila that Patsy had broken her two back legs and cracked a rib, but that she would recover fully and return to her "old dog self" in four to six months, give or take a limp.

"Old dog self?" Sheila said.

"You know," the doctor said, smiling a beat too late, as though she had to remind herself to do it. "Happy, bouncing."

When she got back home, Sheila phoned Colin at his office. "Patsy tried to kill herself."

"What?" Colin said, adjusting his voice. It was hard for him to be in two places at once. He worked as an investigator for a law firm, and was used to people shutting doors in his face and threatening to call the police. This created a tentative quality to his daily demeanor, as if he were speaking while walking quickly away. He had been about to leave Sheila for a woman in Seattle when Sheila discovered the problem with her heart.

"She jumped off a cliff," Sheila said.

"You mean she fell?"

"She leaped, Colin. She just leaped!" When she said the words, she felt something open up inside her.

"I don't understand," Colin said carefully. "Is she okay?"

"I guess it's a matter of how you define 'okay,' " Sheila said.

Colin was silent for a moment. "Can we talk about this later?" he said, finally.

"Of course," she said. Ever since he had told her about his affair and she'd had her surgery, they had tacitly agreed to inhabit a postponed space between "now" and "then," when discussions would be had and decisions made. Their marriage felt like the waiting room at the vet's office—everyone trapped in an expectant tense.

*   *   *

When Sheila was young, her mother told her not to go looking for trouble, but that didn't seem to be good advice. How
else would you find it? She envied the boys she knew for
whom trouble came in the form of discrete activities. You
could steal a car. You could get someone pregnant. You could
become a small-time drug dealer in your neighborhood and be
able to go to all the best concerts. Boy trouble produced a lot of
noise and fuss and trips to the police station. Sheila didn't really want to drink her parents' liquor or break into a stranger's
house and rearrange the pictures on the walls. These journeys
to peril were round-trips; you always ended up the same person you had been before. Girl trouble, on the other hand, was
transformative. You could be driven home by a father after a
babysitting gig and let him touch your breasts. You could have
a fight with your boyfriend and get out of his car on a lonely
road and be picked up by a stranger. You could have sex with
a boy in his dorm room while his roommates walked in and
and out.

Colin had showed up at her door five years earlier to take
down a statement regarding the lawsuit one of her colleagues
had brought against the school district. The teacher's name
was Frank Gibbons, and he had been fired midsemester after
he had left hydrochloric acid out on the lab table overnight.
This was his third offense. Colin was collecting information,
he said, because the district had to be very careful when they
terminated a teacher, especially if that teacher were a minority.

"Frank is white," she said.

"He has a false leg."

"I didn't know that," Sheila said, intrigued. "Was he in the war?"

"I'm not at liberty to disclose more information," Colin said.

Colin's tall and muscled body was squeezed into an ill-fitting suit, which made him appear awkward. Sheila answered his questions, which weren't interesting enough: How long had she known Mr. Gibbons? Did she have any particular dealings with Mr. Gibbons? Had any students ever spoken to her about Mr. Gibbons in her capacity as guidance counselor? He didn't ask whether or not she thought Frank Gibbons suffered from Asperger's, or if he ate the same exact lunch every day—a green apple quartered and a crustless tuna fish sandwich. Colin didn't ask whether she thought he had nefarious intentions when he left the acid lying on the table, knowing that Vanessa LaConte, the remote but brilliant junior with skin the color of espresso beans, would be coming in early the next morning to work on her advanced placement lab. In fact, the interview was over within a few minutes. Colin clicked his pen and handed her his card.

"What should I do with this?" she said.

"In case there is anything else you can think of," Colin said, stiffly. "And, well, you know, it's policy."

"Policy?"

"To identify myself."

Three months later, he arrived again at her door. "They settled the case," he said.

"In favor of?"

"The school district."

"So, he didn't have a leg to stand on, so to speak."

"It was a farm tractor accident."

There was something unsettlingly straightforward about Colin. He was like a toy robot that hits a wall over and over again because all it knows how to do is go forward. She was thirty-two and was attracted to wily men. One had stolen a purse from a street vendor and given it to her as a present. Another asked her to wash herself before sex. She would learn that Colin was not good at innuendo and that he was easily hurt by sarcasm, but by that time, she had fallen in love.

"You broke my heart," she said to Colin through the oxygen mask as the paramedics carried her out of the restaurant where their meal had been interrupted by her sense that an elephant had stepped on her chest. Colin ran alongside the stretcher, clutching her purse, which looked comically small in his big, ex-quarterback hands. She wished she hadn't made the joke, because now it would be another thing between them that was misunderstood, like monogamy. At dinner, he'd told her of his affair with a woman he had known in college. They had reconnected on the Internet, he'd said, shaking his head as if he had been kidnapped by the wonder of technology. The woman was divorced with two kids. Sheila asked to see a picture of the children.

Colin hesitated. "It's over," he said. "I'm not going to see her anymore."

But suddenly her request felt crucial. It was the only concrete thing she could think of to do or say, the only way to gain some purchase on this new unsteady terrain of her life. Unhappily, he reached across the table to show her a picture he'd taken on his cell phone during one of his secret trips to Washington. The children were adorable, with hair so blond you could see sunlight reflected on the top of their heads. Sheila could imagine Colin's lover taking the picture, her smile upsetting the camera so that the image was off-kilter. In Sheila's job at the high school, she sometimes used felt boards and generic family member cutouts to help the kids access their feelings. You could arrange the pieces any way you wanted. The students thought the game was childish but that was the point. As she gazed at the photo on the phone, Sheila began to feel strange, as if all the cells of her body were performing a square dance and were changing partners.

"I don't understand what's happening to me," she said, as she grabbed her left breast.

After Colin finished work, he and Sheila drove to the veterinarian's office to visit Patsy. The dog wore splints on her hind legs, and lay inert in her cage. Colin started to cry.

"Oh shit," he said. "I'm sorry."

"It's normal," the vet said.

"She just looks so helpless," Colin said, smearing his nose with the sleeve of his shirt.

"You love your dog," the vet said, her hand finding her throat and dandling the necklace there. Sheila checked to see whether Colin noticed this gestural flirtation, but he was staring mournfully at Patsy.

He was still upset on the drive home. "Dogs don't commit suicide," he said. "You're a guidance counselor. Didn't you study stuff like this?"

"I work in a school, not the zoo."

"Animals are . . . they just want food. They want to live. It's evolution!" He said this with anguish, as if he had come to the limit of what he could understand. Sheila imagined how flummoxed he must have felt to find himself in a situation of having a mistress with two children who wanted him to take their smiling pictures.

"We give Patsy her food," she said. "She doesn't have to think about hunting and gathering. Her survival is assured."

"So?"

"She's got time on her hands. She thinks about what her purpose is in life. She comes up empty."

"I don't know, Sheila," Colin said, doubtfully.

She felt great affection for the limit of his emotional opacity, even as she knew she had been hurt by it.

She looked over at him thoughtfully. "I know you don't," she said.

She had never given much consideration to her heart until someone had reached inside her and touched it. After the operation, the doctor explained to her that three of her arteries had been eighty percent blocked; it was astonishing that she wasn't already dead. She listened woozily as Colin asked questions about her recovery and prognosis. He wrote down all the answers, asking the doctor to repeat certain phrases, the way he did when he was conducting an investigation. The doctor was young, and Sheila could sense that he was growing nervous in the face of Colin's precision. She wanted to tell the doctor that Colin was an adulterer in order to mitigate Colin's threat, but she couldn't make her mouth work.

"Can she still have kids?" Colin said, shyly.

"Let's see how she does," the doctor said, and left the room.

Why had he asked that question? Was he seeking some kind of justification? A doctor's note like the ones the kids forged in school to get out of PE? But she knew Colin was not capable of such cruelty, and that he was asking for her sake, because he knew that a child was something she wanted, even though, together, they had not managed it.

Colin was constant during her recovery. Sometimes she expressed dismay, her discomfort and bedridden boredom compelling her to pick at the scab of his infidelity. She brought up moral relativism, which she knew was unkind. She remembered when Trudy had taken it upon herself to teach Sheila vocabulary as if three-syllable words were the armor Sheila needed to get by in the world. "Quixotic!" Trudy would scream and Sheila would have three seconds in which to give a definition. Colin withstood Sheila's petulance with calm, implacable smiles, something she imagined he'd learned from his job. His size came in handy as she needed to be carried up and down the stairs of their house until she was strong enough to do so on her own. He brought her food and washed her hair. They sat in bed together night after night and watched infomercials. He traced his hand down the vertical scar that bisected her torso and, two months after the surgery, he made love to her carefully. They did not talk about the woman in Seattle. The tension of the unspoken caused Sheila and Colin to become familiar to one another in a new way, as if they were prisoners of war, sharing a cell and a meager bowl of rice, listening for the footfalls that might seal their fates. When she began dating Colin, she announced to him that if he ever cheated on her, she would leave. But it turned out this was not true. Hurt was not such an obvious thing, and happiness was still more obscure. Her marriage had become perilous and strange, and she felt as she had as a younger woman, when the roommates passed through the room where she and her boyfriend made love. Colin's adultery exposed her desire, turned it into something both pornographic and banal, private and essential.

For the first two weeks after Patsy's surgery, the dog could not move. Still, she tried, starting at the hysterical yips of the neighborhood dogs greeting passing trucks or the sound of the mailbox squeaking open and closed, her instinct trumping the pain of her broken body. Patsy could do nothing for herself, and Sheila had to lift her and carry her outside to do her business. The process was awkward and messy, but Sheila didn't mind. In the afternoons, when she came home from the school, she sat on the floor next to the dog bed and stared into Patsy's large, wet eyes, wondering what had drawn Patsy toward nothingness.

By the third week, Sheila resumed working full-time. On Monday, she sat in her school office across from Morton Washburn. He was a long, angular boy who wore his hair across one eye like a slash of black felt pen marking a grammatical error. Having shed the previous year's gothic persona complete with black fingernails and white-powdered face, he now affected a prep-school style completely out of place in his inner-city high school—deck shoes and square black-framed glasses, collared shirts peeking up above sherbet-colored crewneck sweaters. The burden of his name was so great that he had to work with extra ingenuity in order to turn it from blight into irony. Sheila noted that he insisted on being called Morton rather than Morty, an affectation she thought shrewd.

Morton came to speak to her nearly once a week. He was doing well in school and had not gotten into any trouble. He came from an intact home and his parents always showed up for conferences and signed his report cards. He never had much to say at their sessions, but Sheila felt he was working his way up to telling her he was gay. There were times when she wanted to give him a nudge so that they could get on with it, but instead she sat patiently each week while he tried to manufacture problems that needed her attention. This week, he was having a failure of imagination and they stared across her desk at one another in silence.

"My dog tried to kill herself," she said, finally.

"But why?" he asked. "Was she sad?"

"Define your terms," she said.

Morton sucked in a breath of air. Sheila saw the spark that students got when they matched what they knew to what was being demanded of them and found themselves equal to it. "Despondent, rueful, sorrowful."

"Someone's been studying for his SATs," she said.

He shrugged off an embarrassed smile. "Are you sure she didn't just fall?"

"No. It was intentional. I was there."

"God," Morton said. "Poor baby."

"Do you ever think of hurting yourself, Morton?" she asked. She was supposed to ask such questions when a student expressed anxiety or depression in order to estimate the element of risk. If a student didn't want to discuss such things with her directly, there was a computerized phone intake they could access. A recorded voice asked: Are you taking any drugs? Press 1 for "yes," 2 for "no." Have you considered suicide? Press 1 for "yes," 2 for "no."

"No," Morton said, wearily, as if even that option would not solve things for him. She believed him. It was the ones who proclaimed the impossibility of such an idea whom she worried about.

"Anything else you want to tell me today?" she asked.

"Not really. I feel a lot better, though. I'm glad your dog is okay."

She started to question his assertion but stopped herself. Morton was hesitantly searching for a single answer to the complicated question of himself. Perhaps it would frighten him to know that it was possible to be okay and not okay at the same time, that a thing—a dog, say, or yearning—could only exist alongside the possibility of its absence.

"I like your colors," she said, waving generally at his shirt and sweater as they both stood.

"I just can't wear what everybody else wears," he said, looking down at his chest with anguish.

"It's hard to be a style icon," she said.

"Thank you," he said, relieved.

In February, winter settled in decisively. The afternoon sun was low, and the lights in the houses on the street shone with a kind of menace, as if to say that warmth was locked away. Sheila and Colin unloaded grocery bags from the car while Patsy gamboled in the hedges by the side of the driveway. Sheila watched as her husband hoisted two bags and settled them into his arms like twins. She thought about the man at the lemonade stand, about the secret hidden inside his wrinkled bag. She realized that he could not have had interview clothes in the bag because they would have been wrinkled too.

She had not thought of that when she was younger. She had not fully understood the danger of his desire. She stared at Colin.

"Oh, my God," she said.

"What?" Colin said. "Are you okay?"

"You're going to hurt me, aren't you? You're going to leave."

Colin looked pained. "I love her. I'm sorry."

His clarity rendered her speechless. How could she have known that the bad thing she would never recover from would be love?

The vet was right. Patsy returned to her normal self. Bouncing and happy. Her hair had grown back in the places where she'd been shaved for the surgery. Sheila took her for a long walk, along the steady path of the same development they'd gone to that autumn day. Now the two of them benefited from the smoothness of paved walkways, the gentle ups and downs, Patsy with her gimpy leg, Sheila with her heart. It was April now, but there had been a spring snow the night before. The sun splashed on the white so that Sheila had to avert her watering eyes. She walked Patsy to the embankment and watched the stream below, which moved quickly, hastened by the snowmelt. Patsy put her nose to the ground to sniff at the tough, determined growth that poked through the winter-hardened crust of earth. Sheila had not put Patsy on a leash; she was not worried the dog would jump. Patsy had already taken her leap.

Earlier that day during school Sheila had seen Morton in the hallway. He was talking to Vanessa LaConte. Vanessa carried the flesh of her late childhood with her into adolescence just in case, as though she had overpacked, not knowing what she would need. Sheila remembered her ridiculous fantasy about Vanessa discovering the beaker full of acid. All she wanted now was for the girl to emerge from her childhood unscathed, for no one to hurt her, or even try. She was pleased to see her talking to Morton. But when he leaned down to kiss her on the mouth, Sheila had to stop herself from calling out, "No! No!" as if they had stepped into the path of a bullet. She walked past them, careful not to embarrass them by acknowledging that she had seen them or that she knew Morton in any particular way. And did she know him? She had been certain he would not want to kiss girls. But maybe she was wrong. Or maybe she would eventually be right. She turned a corner feeling suddenly happy, her heart full of a radiant possibility. There was so much time between now and eventually. There was so much trouble yet to come.

The Visitor

. . . .

THE NEW BOY WAS THREE-QUARTERS GONE. BOTH LEGS FROM below the knee and the left arm at the shoulder. Candy spent her lunch hour lying on the lawn outside the VA hospital, sending nicotine clouds into the cloudless sky, wondering whether it would be better to have one leg and no arms—or, if you were lucky enough to have an arm and a leg left, whether it would be better to have them on opposite sides for balance. In her six months as a nurse's aide, she had become thoughtful about the subtle hierarchy of human disintegration. Blind versus deaf—that was a no-brainer, no brain being perhaps the one wound in her personal calculus that could not be traded in for something worse.

It was sad. Of course it was sad. But she didn't feel sad. Sad was what people said they were in the face of tragedies as serious as suicide bombings or as minor as a lost earring. It was a word that people used to tidy up and put the problem out of sight.

The grass was making needle-like pricks through the thin material of her maroon scrubs, and she sat up, smoothing her matching V-neck over her chest and belly, feeling the familiar stab of self-consciousness as her hand rode over the unfashionable lumps. In photographs, Candy's mother, Sylvie, was as skinny as dripping water at age twenty-two, but that could have been a result of the drugs. Candy had her grandmother's build, and she knew that as the years passed her shape would settle into the short, hale block that was Marjorie, less body than space-saver.

Candy glanced at her watch. She still had ten minutes left until the end of her break.

She wasn't sure when she had last felt sad. She knew that she must have been sad when she was eleven and her mother had gone into the hospital for the last time. But she couldn't actually recall the feeling. She did remember being happy afterward, sitting at her grandmother's kitchen table picking walnuts out of their shells with the tines of a fork while Marjorie made phone calls to let people know that Sylvie had landed on her final and terminal addiction: death. She listened to Marjorie say, "My baby *diiihd*," the last vestiges of her Texas accent breathing so much air into the word that Candy could almost see it flying up toward the ceiling of the kitchen like a helium balloon. Sylvie's presence in Candy's life had been birdlike. She would swoop into Marjorie's apartment from time to time to drop a Big Mac into Candy's waiting mouth, but the enthusiasm that she'd carried with her usually dissipated quickly, smothered as much by Marjorie's insistence on behaving as if nothing were out of the ordinary as by Candy's abject need.

Candy recalled feeling another sort of happiness, too, when she had crawled over the railing of the hospital bed in order to lie next to her mother one last time. Marjorie had forced Candy to wear a new party dress she'd sewn the day before. Made with leftover material from the flower-girl frock that Marjorie had been working on, it was an embarrassing pink affair that grabbed at the tender buds of Candy's breasts with tight smocking. What was the point, Candy had whined, as Marjorie finished off the hem, breathing heavily through her nose, her mouth a cactus of pins. But in the hospital, lying beside her mother, Candy had understood why she was so dressed up: she was there to act out the role of daughter in the hope that Sylvie would wake and finally take up her own part in the charade of parenting that Marjorie had insisted on whenever Sylvie showed up at the apartment—as if Sylvie had come back not for food or a shower or money but to French-braid Candy's hair or to explain menstruation to her. The metal guardrails on the bed had felt cold against Candy's thighs. The sensation was shocking in a pleasurable way that she couldn't name then, but it wasn't long before she discovered that the faucet in her grandmother's bathtub could be angled to hit her between the legs just so.

When Candy first started working at the VA, the other aides had said that it would take her a long time to get "used to it." They'd told her to look away from the wounds, to focus on the soldiers' faces as a way to protect the boys from embarrassment and herself from disgust. But she was not disgusted, even when she had to rewrap stumps or sponge gashes that were sewn up like shark bites. She found these molestations frankly interesting, the body deconstructed so that you could see what it really was: just bits and pieces, no different from the snatches of fabric that Marjorie wrestled into dresses for Mr. Victor of Paris, the tailor in Burbank who had employed her for thirty-seven years. The nurses praised Candy's bravery, but when she passed by a group of aides taking their break in the cafeteria one afternoon, she knew from their covert glances that they found her strange. She once overheard a girl say that she had no heart.

Well, no heart was better than no brain, Candy thought, as she sucked on the last of her cigarette and stubbed it out in the grass, dismissing the notion that she might cause a brushfire in this hottest of seasons. She knew that hers was not a singular life, that she would not be the cause of anything monumental. Recently the thermometer had topped out at a hundred and nine in the valley. The power had failed in her grandmother's apartment complex, where Candy had lived all her life. Marjorie, excited by the idea of a disaster that she might have some control over, had instructed Candy to gather her important papers, as if she expected the apartment to burst into spontaneous flames. Candy scanned the top of her dresser, where her community college diploma sat in its Plexiglas frame alongside assorted gift-with-purchase tubes of lipstick and miniature eyeshadow compacts. In a gesture that even at the time she regarded as TV-movie maudlin, she put her mother's Communion cross around her neck and lay down on her bed. When she was woken by the sudden snap of lights turning on and the sound of her window fan whirring to life, she took off the necklace and placed it back in her dresser drawer. She showered and went to bed naked, letting the fan blow its slow, oscillating wind across her body.

The new boy's name was Gregorio Villalobos. Juana, the admitting nurse, told Candy that *lobo* meant "wolf" in Spanish. Down the hall lay a Putter and a Shooter, boys who clung to their jaunty monikers as though they were one day going to walk out of the hospital and back onto the golf course or the basketball court where they had earned those nicknames. Candy wondered if the new boy had been called El Lobo in the service. She could ask him, but he wouldn't answer her. He had not yet spoken. He watched her as she moved around the room, his eyes tracking her as if she were a fly and he was waiting for the right moment to bring down his swatter. Most of the boys looked at her when she brought them food or checked IV bags, but their gazes were like those of old dogs: hope combined with the absence of hope. The nurses chattered at the boys as they went about their work, talking about the weather or whatever sports trivia they had picked up from their husbands. In general, the boys went along with this, and Candy often felt as if she were watching a play in which all the actors had agreed to pretend that someone onstage had not just taken a huge shit. Candy knew that the nurses were scared of silence, and perhaps the boys were, too.

Before she left the room, she looked at El Lobo's chart. It wasn't her business to read charts, simply to mark down what he did and didn't eat, did and didn't expel. She'd received minimal training, most of which had to do with things that anyone who'd ever cleaned a house would know and she couldn't understand much of what was written on the chart. But she did understand the phrase "elective muteness." She stared at El Lobo, feeling words crawling up inside her, pushing to get past her closed lips—that pathetic human need to communicate when there was nothing to say. She had been this way when her mother was alive. On the occasions when Sylvie was home, Candy had told her anything she could think of to say: what had happened at school that day, what clothing the popular girls were wearing, how pretty she thought Sylvie looked, with her dark hair parted down the center and hanging on either side of her narrow face like a magician's cape. She'd talk and talk, and the more she suspected that her mother didn't care what she was saying, the more she'd fill the apartment with her desperate noise.

She replaced the chart on the hook at the foot of the bed and glanced at El Lobo once more before leaving the room. She could be silent longer than he could. He had no idea who he was dealing with.

That night she woke to the sound of her grandmother yelling at the ghost. "Get outta here *rii-ght* this minute!" Marjorie said, her accent always thicker when she was torn from her dreams, as if her unconscious resided in Beaumont, Texas, while the rest of her kept pace in L.A. Water splashed noisily against the porcelain sink in the bathroom between Candy's and Marjorie's bedrooms.

Candy lay in her bed, which had been her mother's childhood bed, the headboard still bearing the Day-Glo flower stickers her mother had affixed to it. Candy tried to imagine Sylvie as a naïve girl who liked stickers, but it was impossible.

What she remembered most about her mother was the patchouli scent of her skin, underneath which hid a more elusive, dirty smell, an odor that Candy yearned to excavate whenever Sylvie was near. But Sylvie did not often let her daughter get that close. Even during the times when she was living at home, when she swore to Marjorie that she was clean, and Marjorie decided, all pinny-eyed, fidgety evidence to the contrary, to believe her, Sylvie kept herself apart. She'd take over her old room, leaving Candy to the sofa in the living room, and Candy would spend the early-evening hours inventing reasons to walk past the bedroom door, hoping that it might open, that she might be invited in.

Candy listened as her grandmother hurried into the bathroom to turn off the faucet.

"Turn that water on again and I'll murder you!" Marjorie said to the ghost, on her way past Candy's room to the kitchen. "It's quarter past three, for Lord's sake."

Candy got out of bed and made her way to the kitchen, too. Marjorie wore her quilted bathrobe, and her bulb of short graying hair was lopsided from lying in bed. She had already set the kettle on the stove. "Ah, she woke you up, too," she said, shaking her head ruefully.

"*You* woke me up," Candy said, sitting down at the table. "You probably woke the whole building."

"That ghost is running up my water bill. It has to stop."

"Maybe he's thirsty," Candy said.

"He's a she, and ghosts don't drink, darlin'. They have no bodies. She just turns on the tap to get my goat. *And in a dry season, no less!*" she yelled, shaking her fist in the air, as if the ghost were hiding just outside the kitchen door. The wattle beneath Marjorie's upper arm wavered and Candy remembered how she had played with that loose skin as a child. Something about her grandmother's excesses of flesh was comforting. On bad nights, when Candy felt an aching maw open up in her chest, she'd slip into Marjorie's bed. Her nameless dread was always calmed when her cheeks grazed the loose bags of her grandmother's nylon-swaddled breasts.

Marjorie set down two mugs on the kitchen table, then brought over the kettle and poured. "I'll tell you what, though. I'm tired of waking up in the middle of the night. I'm too old for it."

"Maybe we should have an exorcism."

"You don't believe in that foolishness, I hope." She saw Candy's grin. "Oh, you're just teasing me, you bad girl."

"We got a new boy in," Candy said, changing the subject. "He's a mess."

"Ahh," Marjorie said, sympathetically, replacing the kettle on the stove.

"No one's come to visit him. It's been two days."

"Maybe he has no one."

"They're usually there at admitting with their balloons and those smiles. You can see them counting the minutes until they can get the hell out of there."

"You're harsh, baby girl. It's not easy to see something destroyed."

Candy looked at her grandmother's hands. Arthritis, that devious sculptor, was beginning to shape them, and it wouldn't be long before she could no longer work a sewing machine or hold needle and thread. What then? Could they survive on Marjorie's Social Security and Candy's pathetic salary? Candy remembered Marjorie's younger, stronger hands cupping Sylvie's cheeks as she tried to wake her, tried to get her to stand up from the living-room floor where she had collapsed sometime during the night. "Time to get your girl to school!" Marjorie would say, her determination fending off the futility of her effort. Candy remembered, too, her grandmother's callused grip around her own small hand when they made those hurried journeys to school together, more often than not leaving Sylvie behind, curled up on herself like a pill bug.

El Lobo was, of course, where Candy had left him the afternoon before, lying in his bed, gazing up at the ceiling. She raised the mattress so that he faced forward, placed his breakfast tray on the rolling table, and swung it across the bed. She removed the lid from the oatmeal and the canned pears and peeled off the layer of plastic wrap covering the glass of water. The meal's monchromatic paleness was disheartening, but Candy dug into the oatmeal with a spoon and lifted it to El Lobo's mouth. He ate dutifully but without affect, as if some inner computer chip were responsible for the opening and closing of his lips and the gentle modulations of his throat. He made no eye contact with her. Candy took the opportunity to go vacant as well, a state she had perfected as a child. She'd found that she could continue to do what was required of her—clean her room or go through the motions of paying attention in class, even read out loud if the teacher requested it—while her mind wandered. In that peaceful oblivion, she felt swaddled in cotton, divorced from the feelings that usually plagued her, unworried about what she looked like in her homemade clothing or what others thought of the girl with a grandmother for a mother. The sounds of her fellow students came at her muffled, harmless. Time passed. She disappeared.

She looked over to find that El Lobo's chin was covered with syrup where she had missed his mouth. It irked her that he had let this happen without making any sound to alert her to the problem. She wiped him clean, becoming even more irritated when he didn't seem to register this help either. She took a last, hard swipe at his mouth. He finally looked at her, and his glance was sharp and full of menace. The ease with which his expression resolved into hatred made it clear that anger was his default position. The nurses talked about the "sweet" boys or the "darling" boys, as if the upside of the physical damage were that it turned a soldier into a feckless three-year-old, thus ridding the world of one more potentially dangerous man. But Candy knew that this boy was neither sweet nor darling and probably never had been. She imagined him as a bored high-school shark, moving slow and silent through the halls, heavy with his own power and cravings. She had known boys like this, had fucked boys like this.

She marked on his chart the amount of solids and liquids he had consumed, rolled the tray away from his bed, and carried the half-eaten breakfast into the hallway. She spent the next seven hours of her shift changing sheets and emptying bedpans, delivering food baskets that would be at the nurses' station by day's end, as most of the patients were on restricted diets or were fed through tubes. She wheeled one boy to X-ray through the maze of hallways and elevators. Every time the gurney lurched over a transom the boy winced in pain. The first few times she apologized, but then she stopped because she knew that her regret, like a basket of muffins, was, in some way, an affront.

Later that day, after she had finished her shift, she returned to El Lobo's room. He was asleep, so she sat in the orange plastic chair in the corner and watched him. When he lay in his bed covered in blankets, his wounds were invisible; his head, his nutmeg skin, his thick, dark eyebrows and generous, scowling mouth were untouched. A stranger might have thought him one of the lucky ones in this war. Only after his so-called recovery, when he would have to have special clothing made, when he would be assaulted by all the daily acts he could no longer accomplish, would he truly feel the extent of his wounds. She knew about collateral damage, knew that the injuries people saw were never the gravest. After Sylvie died, the school counselor had brought Candy into her office and handed her a pamphlet called "Teen-Agers and Grief: A Handbook." She'd told Candy that although it was against state regulations she was going to give Candy a hug. She'd had no idea about the hard lump of rage that sat lodged in Candy's throat like a nut swallowed whole.

After fifteen minutes, El Lobo's eyes opened. For a second, his expression was soft and pliable like that of a child waking from a nap, but then his mind took over and something calcified in his features, his muscles hardening against the invasion of thought. His gaze fell on her. She didn't move, but continued to stare at him. He stared back, his upper lip trembling in what she thought was the beginning of an insult. She felt a tingling in her gut, and her nerves were on alert, as if he had actually grazed her skin with that leftover hand. The second-shift nurse's voice cut through the silence as she entered and exited rooms along the hallway, announcing pain-relieving meds in a voice as bright and cutting as a laser. Candy stood and walked over to the bed. She reached under the cover and pinched El Lobo hard on his arm. She heard his sharp intake of breath, and slipped out of the room before she was discovered.

At 3 a.m., Marjorie tore into the bathroom. "You leave me alone!" she yelled. "I've done enough for you already." Candy decided to stay in bed. A few times, over the five years since the ghost had announced itself, Candy had tried to stay up all night. She thought that if she could just once catch Marjorie turning on the faucet—perhaps it was sleepwalking or some early sign of senility—her grandmother would stop the nonsense, and Candy could get some rest. But on those nights either the ghost did not appear or Candy dropped off to sleep despite the cans of Coke littering her bedside table.

She heard the sound of the sewing machine clattering into action. The machine slowed and quickened, and Candy imagined her grandmother's bare foot playing the floor pedal. Candy knew that she had little chance of getting back to sleep. It was too hot to put on her terry-cloth robe, so, wearing only her T-shirt and underwear, she went into the living room, where Marjorie bent to her task.

"What are you making?" Candy said.

"Right about now: nothing," Marjorie said. She lifted the foot of the sewing machine and pulled the material out, snipped the threads with a pair of scissors, and set to undoing her work. "Victor gives me two weeks to do a bride and four bridesmaids. Two weeks! The man is losing whatever brains he had to begin with."

Candy watched her grandmother's hands shake as she pulled out the tiny stitches with her seam ripper. Marjorie was no longer as adept as she had been when she was younger and able to unroll a bolt of cloth and see every seam and dart, every buttonhole and facing, when she could tell, even before putting one pin into the material, how it would all fall together. A dress form stood beside the sewing machine, draped in the raw ivory silk that Marjorie was working with. Headless and armless, the figure tilted slightly on its stand, as if leaning over to tell a secret.

"Expensive," Candy said, fingering the cloth.

"Hands off!" Marjorie ordered, batting Candy's hands away lightly as she had done when Candy was young. "Spend all this money on silk and then give me next to no time to do my job. This missy will be lucky if the whole thing doesn't come flying apart the minute she starts down the aisle."

"Where's the ghost?"

"Gone, that wretched thing. She'll be back, though. What I ever did to deserve a hauntin', I'll never know."

"Maybe she lived here. Before us. Maybe she wants her place back."

"And it's taken her thirty-five years to show up? Unh-unh."

"What, then?"

"Honey, I'm still trying to figure out the reason people do what they do when they're alive." She finished ripping out the stitches, sighed audibly, and fit the material into the machine again.

Candy went to the window and looked out over the apartment courtyard. The management had recently overhauled the space, taking out the grass and flowers that had required watering and replacing them with decorative pebbles. Only the concrete path that wound through the garden remained. As a child, Candy had ridden her bike between clumps of impatiens and begonia and stands of banana trees, clumsy with their thick, waxy leaves. She knew every turn and straight-away by heart, but there had been danger inherent in each corner, the thrill of heading into the unseen. She'd been eight when she'd made a turn around a bushel of bamboo and saw her mother lying asleep across the doormat of Marjorie's apartment. Candy parked her bike against the wall and squat-ted down next to Sylvie. She looked pretty lying there, like the illustration of Sleeping Beauty in one of Candy's library books. Candy watched her for a while as if studying an insect, noting the little flutters of her eyelids and lips, her long, corded neck, the muscles of which seemed tense, even in sleep. Finally, she stepped over her mother and went inside.

"Mommy's back," she told Marjorie, who was bent over her machine.

Together, they carried an incoherent and moaning Sylvie into the bathroom. Candy sat on the lid of the toilet while Marjorie ran the bath, undressed her daughter, and coaxed her into the water. Sylvie cursed her mother, calling her a bitch and a cunt, but Marjorie didn't react, only shushed her the way she shushed Candy when she was crying over a scraped knee as if silence trumped pain. Once Sylvie was in the bath, she lay with her eyes closed, head back against the edge of the tub, while Marjorie gently soaped her body, lifting her arms one by one, cleaning between her small breasts and her legs. "Beautiful girl," she sang in an errant, unidentifiable tune. "Beautiful baby girl." Later, the three ate chicken with mushroom-soup sauce at the kitchen table and watched MTV on the twenty-one-inch Sony. In the morning, Sylvie was gone, along with the television.

The apartment was reduced bit by bit over the following years. The microwave followed the television, and then some of Marjorie's jewelry disappeared. Each time Candy came back to the apartment after school she entered with trepidation, waiting to discover what was missing. The relief she felt when she realized that Sylvie had not stolen anything new was always tempered by disappointment. When she and Marjorie arrived home from church one Sunday to find the space where the stereo had sat looking as vacant as a missing tooth, Candy felt a rush of elation. Her mother had been in the apartment. Her breath, her dirty, pretty smell still hung in the air. Marjorie never got angry about the thefts. She'd just stand, hands on hips, facing the emptiness, and inhale deeply as if acquainting herself with the new geography of her life.

But when Candy was ten and she and Marjorie returned from the grocery store to find that Marjorie's black Singer Featherweight, the hand-me-down from her mother and grandmother that she had oiled and massaged and kept going for years, was gone, Marjorie went to her bedroom and didn't come out until the following morning. Candy heated up a can of alphabet soup and sat on the couch waiting for Marjorie to show her how to skirt this new boulder in her life, but her grandmother didn't open her door.

"Are you mad?" Candy asked the next morning, when Marjorie finally came out of her room, her face blotchy.

Marjorie fingered the thin pages of the phone book, looking for the number of a locksmith. "I'm just tired," she said softly. Two weeks later, Marjorie held Candy's hand at the kitchen table as they listened to Sylvie struggle to turn her key in the front-door lock.

"I know you're in there!" Sylvie yelled, pounding on the door.

Candy looked at Marjorie, who held her finger to her lips,

and the two sat in rigid silence. Giving up on the door, Sylvie came to the kitchen window. She pressed her pallid and wild-eyed face up to the glass so that her nose and lips flattened and distorted.

"Let her in, Grandma. Please," Candy said.

"We don't want any visitors just now," Marjorie said.

For the next year, until her mother's death, Candy often had the feeling of being shadowed, as if a huge prehistoric bird were passing over her, but when she looked up there was nothing there.

El Lobo had his eyes closed when Candy brought in his breakfast the next day, but she knew he wasn't asleep—there was something too effortful about his breathing. Noisily, she set up the tray table and dragged her chair to the side of his bed. When he finally opened his eyes, he stared at the opposite wall. This time, she did not feed him but simply sat and waited for him to say something. He did not move or shift his gaze. The air in the room grew heavy with tension, but neither one gave in. After ten minutes, Candy rolled the table away from the bed and took the uneaten food from the room. In the hallway, she met up with Tammy, the floor nurse.

"What happened?" Tammy said, eying the uneaten food.

"He's not hungry."

"He said this?" Tammy asked, warily.

"He made it clear."

"He spoke?"

"He wasn't hungry," Candy repeated. "I'm not supposed to force-feed."

"Well," Tammy said, considering, "did you mark it down?"

Candy nodded. "Zero in. Zero out."

"It's bath time, anyway. Give me some help."

After gathering supplies and filling a small bowl with warm water, Candy came back into El Lobo's room. Tammy leaned over the bed and pulled El Lobo toward her. "Candy, get the tie," she said.

Candy put down her supplies and came around the bed. She saw El Lobo's dark skin where the hospital gown split open in the back. A fine down feathered away from his spine. She resisted the urge to touch that fur. She undid the tie and watched while Tammy gently laid El Lobo back against his pillows, then drew the gown down past his shoulders and chest. The dressing that covered the wound where his arm had been was secured by white bandages that stretched across his breastbone, contrasting with his dark skin and his nearly black nipples.

"We're just going to do a little spa treatment!" Tammy said loudly. "How's that?"

El Lobo said nothing and Tammy chattered on, explaining that they would not be taking off his dressing but would just wash around it to freshen him up, and that the doctor would be in later to see how he was doing, and wasn't he doing well, Candy? Good color in his face. Like he's been to the beach! Have you been sneaking out of here and hitting the beach? Ha-ha-ha. All the while she sponged his chest, neck, and face, and then, reaching down under the blanket with the warm cloth, her head turned to the side as if to control her urge to look, Tammy cleaned him off below. Candy doled out fresh, damp cloths and took away the used ones, then held a bowl under El Lobo's mouth while Tammy brushed his teeth. Spit! Good one! Spit again! They dressed him in a clean gown. Hello, gorgeous!

Candy knew just what El Lobo was up to, with his pliant body and immobile gaze. She felt a warm rush of anger start in her stomach and rise into her throat. She wanted to hit him. She wanted to hear him react.

"Candy. We have a situation here."

Candy looked over and watched as a stain spread across the sheet covering El Lobo's lower half.

"That's just a normal thing, honey," Tammy said to El Lobo. "You get that warm water down there and it makes you want to go, right?"

She began to remove the wet sheet covering El Lobo, but her beeper went off. She checked the readout and handed the sheet to Candy. "I'll call for an orderly," she said, and left the room.

Candy looked at El Lobo, whose head was turned away. She left the room, threw the dirty sheet in the laundry chute and got a clean gown and fresh bedding from the supply closet. She looked down the hall for the orderly but no one was coming. She waited next to El Lobo's door. After a few minutes, the orderly still had not come and Candy was angry. Angry at the hospital for making her take care of this when it was not part of her job, angry because El Lobo had to lie there in his own piss and stink. She went to his bed thinking that she would change his tunic first. That would be easy enough to do alone and by the time she was done the orderly would have arrived. But then she realized that if she did not change the bottom sheet first his new gown would become wet, and she'd have to do the whole thing over again. So carefully, as if handling something breakable, she rolled El Lobo onto his good side. He was heavier than she expected a person with most of his body missing to be, and he did nothing to help her. When she stopped pushing, he fell back so that he was prone again. Her frustration with him and his intransigence welled up and she was thinking of leaving, letting him lie in his own mess until the orderly arrived, when she noticed that his eyes were not simply closed but squeezed shut, like those of a child playing hide-and-seek.

Carefully, she pushed him onto his side again, this time bracing herself against his back as she inched the sheet out from under him. It was hard work but she was careful not to make any sounds that would cause him to sense her effort. She reached for a wet towel and quickly swiped it across the mattress, then shook out a clean sheet and managed to slip it underneath him just as he was becoming too heavy for her to hold where he was. She laid him back down and walked around the bed, working the sheet until it lay reasonably flat. Next, she undid his tunic and pulled it from his body. She plunged a washcloth into the bowl of now lukewarm water and gently cleaned him off. She wiped around his belly and his groin, reached under him to get at his backside. His soft, pale penis lay against his thigh as bald as a newborn puppy, but she did not take her eyes away. This was his body. It deserved to be seen. She dressed him in a fresh gown, holding him against her chest as she tied the strings. She knew that she could not grip him by the shoulders to lay him back against his pillows because of his pain there, so she kept her arms around his ribs and leaned him all the way down as if she were embracing him. When she pulled away, his eyes were open, and she saw, for a brief second, the arrow of his hatred for her and for everything that had happened to him bending back on itself and aiming straight into his own heart.

Marjorie was sewing at the machine when the power went out. It was ten o'clock at night, and the darkness was sudden and blinding. For a moment, both Candy and Marjorie froze where they were in the living room.

"Oh, shoot. I'm just in the middle of something, too," Marjorie said, finally. "Get the flashlights."

Candy felt her way down the hall and into the kitchen, struck by how frightening real darkness was. She felt a brief panic rise up. What if the power never came back on? What if they had to grope around in this darkness forever? She turned on the flashlights and brought them into the living room, glad to be near her grandmother again.

"It's getting hotter already," Marjorie said.

Candy opened the windows to the courtyard but when she went to the other side of the room to open the street windows for a cross breeze Marjorie stopped her.

"Thieves," she said. "They just wait for times like this."

Candy could already feel sweat forming in the creases of her underarms and beneath her breasts. She took one of the flashlights and trained it on the thermostat.

"It's already eighty in here."

Marjorie slid the material out from under the foot of the machine. "I guess I'll have to do this by hand if I'm gonna be finished in time. Shine that light over here."

Candy stood above Marjorie and trained her flashlight

onto the pearly white silk. She watched as her grandmother struggled to thread a needle with fingers that were beginning to bend at odd angles like old trees.

"I need glasses," Marjorie said, missing the eye of the needle and wetting the tip of the thread between her lips.

"Want me to do it?" Candy offered.

"I can thread my own needle, thank you. Been doing it more than half my lifetime."

She was successful on the next try, drew out the thread, and tied a knot at the bottom. She adjusted the material on her lap. Candy watched as Marjorie attempted to work the needle through the material in the seed-size stitches required for the seam. The stitches were uneven, and Candy waited for Marjorie to stop or get out her seam ripper but she continued, her breath coming hard out of her nose as she pursed her lips. Candy felt heat rise in her face as she watched her grandmother's awkward, determined work.

"The power will probably come back on soon," Candy said, trying to keep her voice neutral.

"And if it doesn't? I've got a bride here who's not gonna care about my excuses if her dress isn't ready in time."

Candy tried to imagine the bride that her grandmother could see in this material bunched up on her lap. Was she short, tall? Full-breasted or flat? Was her grandmother conjuring up a beauty when the reality was far different?

"What's she like?"

"Who?"

"The bride."

"They're all the same, you know. Just girls. They don't know what's happening to them. Oh! Oh!"

Candy saw the spot of red and snatched the cloth off her

grandmother's lap before the blood could spread any farther on the material. She reached for her grandmother's hand. "Don't move," she said. "I'll get a Band-Aid."

When she returned from the bathroom, Marjorie was standing and holding the wedding dress out in front of her with her good hand so that it fell into its bodiless shape.

"It's pretty," Candy said.

"It's beyond repair."

It was impossible to sleep. Even with the windows open, the air in the bedroom was close, the heat making it almost hard to breathe. Candy lay on top of her covers, her arms and legs spread out so that her skin wouldn't chafe. Marjorie's bedroom door opened. Candy listened as her grandmother went into the bathroom, then she got up quickly. If she was quiet, perhaps she could catch her grandmother turning on the water. But as her hand touched the doorknob, she stopped herself and sat back down on her bed. "Get out! Get out! *Come on, now!*" she heard her grandmother say in the gentle, forgiving tone she'd used when she bathed Sylvie or when Candy touched her sewing material with dirty hands, as if their transgressions didn't really bother her at all, as if she was grateful for the intrusion.

Three Girls

. . . .

CONNIE WAS ALWAYS THE FIRST ONE AWAKE IN THE MORNINGS, and after dressing for school and making her bed, she went downstairs to the kitchen and poured out three bowls of Cheerios, sprinkling a bit of sugar over Paula's so that she wouldn't whine, her complaints threading themselves dangerously up the stairs. It had begun to snow the night before, and there was already an inch of the fine white powder on the windowsills. Jean came into the kitchen. She was seventeen and taller than most girls and some of the boys in the senior class. Connie had heard boys say that Jean had the tits to make up for her awkward height. Paula came downstairs, and the three girls sat to eat. Only Paula had inherited the Nordic genes of their mother, her hair yellow-blond and straight, her face wide and pale. Connie and Jean were dark like their father, with deep-set eyes and the bruised circles below them that were impossible to erase with drugstore cosmetics. Paula played a game of fishing a single Cheerio out of her bowl with her spoon and watching it float in the moat of milk before eating it, as if it were a treasure she'd brought up from the bottom of the ocean. Connie wondered at her younger sister's untroubled ability to commit so fully to every activity. As if you could eat a bowl of cereal or drink a glass of juice and that was all there was to it. When Connie finished her cereal she waited while Paula lifted her bowl to her lips and drank the last of her sweet milk. Then Connie washed and dried the bowls, replacing them in the cupboard and the clean spoons in the silverware drawer. She liked when the kitchen was arranged so you could not tell anyone had been there.

Jean packed Paula's lunch and wiped the dribbles of milk from the table in front of Paula's place. "Pee and brush," she said to Paula.

"I already did," Paula said. She was seven years old.

"Let me smell," Jean said, leaning over her sister. She didn't need to sniff Paula's breath before Paula retreated to the downstairs bathroom.

"She just stands there, you know. At the sink," Connie said. "She doesn't brush."

"I know," Jean said. She slipped into her winter coat.

"Aren't you going to do anything about it?"

"Why should I?" Jean asked as she walked outside. Connie watched through the window as Jean pulled the garbage cans down the drive to the curb. Connie filled Whisper's bowl with kibble. The old hound struggled up from where he was lying by the heating vent, moved slowly to inspect the situation, then lay down again. Jean came back inside with the cold air, her cheeks and hands red. She refused to wear a hat and gloves even on the coldest days of winter.

"He's not eating again," Connie said, staring at the dog. "He needs to go to the vet."

"You worry too much."

"No I don't."

"Yes you do. It's a drag."

Jean glanced toward the stairs, and Connie knew she was thinking about their parents. They would not want to be bothered with Whisper. "He'll eat when he's hungry enough," Jean said. She smiled encouragingly and Connie felt her heart fill with gratitude for her sister. Jean could be mean sometimes, but Connie knew that she was only being sarcastic. When Jean passed her best friend in the hall at school, she'd call out "Hey, slut," and her friend would say "Hey, bitch," but they would be smiling.

Paula came out from the bathroom and Jean handed her the neon green parka that had been her own, and then Connie's. Connie remembered her mother saying she'd chosen the unlikely color so that she could always find her children, as though it were easy to lose them. Connie thought her mother hadn't much cared what color the coat was, and that she had not thought about the fact that her children would be called Caterpillar or Puke when they wore the jacket.

The girls walked down their street in single file along the narrow path that had been cleared by others' footsteps. The snow was not deep enough for the plows yet. Cars drove slowly down the street, and the few people making their way from their homes to the sidewalks moved with careful steps. Connie had the impression that the world had become like an old person overnight, uncertain and expectant of danger. When they reached the elementary school, Paula ran toward the front door along with the other children. Connie tried to remember when she had run just to get someplace a little faster.

All morning long it snowed, and Connie stared out the classroom windows, paying little attention to the lessons. The relentlessness of the storm made the students edgy and impatient, and there was an unfocused excitement in the air. The bells ringing at the end of each period seemed louder and more disruptive than usual, and as the sky darkened, the brightly lit classrooms felt isolated, as if they were boxes of light floating in dark space. Anxiety slid beneath Connie's skin like a worm. She looked for Jean in the hallways during breaks, but she couldn't find her. Finally, a voice came over the PA system and announced that there would be an early dismissal due to the storm. Connie met up with Jean by the front door and together they made their way to Paula's school, heads bent low as if to break through the wall of snow the way explorers might use machetes to cut down tangled brush in a jungle. Connie thought that Jean must be regretting her choice of shoes over boots and her missing hat, but Connie didn't mention it. It was the kind of thing a mother would say, and Connie didn't want Jean to put her down.

The family had attended the faculty Christmas party the night before at the president's house. Connie's parents taught at the local college, and every year, on the evening of the annual event, Connie's mother made the girls dress nicely and reminded them to shake hands and look people in the eye so they wouldn't look like a bunch of scared mice. At the party, the polished wood table was always filled with tureens of eggnog and platters of vegetables that no one ate. Paula got caught up in a game near the Christmas tree with some of the younger children. Connie was about to suggest to Jean that they go find a place to sit and wait out the party, but Jean started talking to a man with a gray goatee who wore a sweater with a snowflake design on it. Jean put her hand on the man's chest so that her palm covered one of the flakes and the man laughed. Connie thought the man was disgusting, but Jean kept talking to him. Maybe Jean was trapped. Sometimes when Connie and Jean were at the mall, they ran into a group of seniors Jean didn't like. Jean would look at Connie, her eyes widening meaningfully, and Connie would make up a lie about being late for her bassoon lesson so as to allow Jean to leave gracefully. Jean would smile conspiratorially as they walked away, and sometimes even offer a furtive high five. Connie wouldn't mind so much that the older girls were probably making fun of the fact that she played the bassoon because she and Jean were a team. Sensing Jean's distress at being cornered by the man with the terrible sweater, Connie tried to think of a good excuse that would allow Jean to save face. But then Jean traced her collarbone with her finger and drew her hand down over her chest and onto her belly. The man's gaze followed along, as if tethered to Jean's hand by a leash.

Even though she wasn't hungry, Connie ate a fistful of baby carrots. Her mother stood at the far end of the table, watching as a man poured a bottle of liquor into the punch bowl. Connie's mother put her glass into the stream. The amber liquid splashed over her skin and she and the man laughed as Connie's mother licked her palm.

Across the room, the younger children were fighting, and Paula burst into tears. She ran to her mother and buried her face in her stomach. Nearby partyers looked over at the commotion. Connie's mother juggled her drink while patting Paula's heaving back, making a phony put-upon expression that was meant to ally her with the other adults in the room. There was always a moment at these parties when Connie's mother's behavior became cartoonish and broad, as if she were reading a storybook to children. Connie felt her jaw ache. She was clenching her teeth the way she did when she took a test at school.

Someone entered the room dressed as Santa and the smaller children took turns sitting on his lap. By this time Paula had calmed down and she leaned into the big man's face, reeling off her list of gifts. Eventually, grown women sat on Santa's lap and there was laughter and knowing hoots. Someone fed Santa a drink that dribbled down his synthetic beard. Connie's mother slid onto Santa's lap and he dipped her back as if he were dancing with her. She was wearing a skirt, and her legs fell open, and Connie could see where her thighs pressed together. When she sat up, someone said "What did you ask for?" and Connie's mother said "I'm not telling!" and someone else whistled. Connie felt her face grow hot with shame.

She found Jean, who was still talking to the man in the sweater. "I think we should leave now," Connie said.

Jean put her arm around Connie's shoulder. "This is my sister who doesn't know how to have fun at a party," Jean said. Connie felt embarrassed but also proud that Jean's arm was around her and that the man was looking at her with interest. Maybe she had saved Jean after all. Later, when they were home, Jean would invite her into her room and tell her all the stupid things this man had said. Her mother's reckless laugh interrupted her thoughts.

"Where's Paula? Did you see where she went?" Connie

said. She looked around the room urgently. She knew they had to leave the party right away. She felt the same queasy sensation she got when she was riding the Tilt-A-Whirl at the county fair and her stomach went the opposite way from the rest of her. She heard her mother's and father's voices cut through the noise in the room, their tone biting and loud. Connie's mother's glass fell to the floor and shattered, shards winking in the spilled liquid like silverfish.

"Get the coats, Connie," Jean said.

On the way home, the girls rode in the back of the old Volvo pressed low in their seat by the weight of their parents' silence. Their mother's head fell back against the headrest, her mascara pooling at the corners of her eyes. Their father strained forward to see past the windshield, as if he were looking for ghosts.

"You made it!" Connie's mother said, when her daughters walked through the door from school. "I was wondering how you girls were going to get home." She had pulled jars from the pantry and lined them up on the kitchen table. There were olives and tomatoes and tubes of anchovy paste. There was Campbell's chicken noodle soup and artichoke hearts and tuna fish, peanut butter and apricot jam. "They closed the college," Connie's mother said. "They've closed the town." She set her glass down and the ice inside it popped. The house smelled like the inside of the glass—a customary odor of sweet, tangy decay that lived in the cushions of the furniture and the curtains. "Snow day!" she said, drawing Paula to her in a hug.

"At school they said it was an emergency!" Paula said, happily.

"It's the best kind of emergency," her mother said. "I love it when everything just stops, don't you?"

They ate dinner at four o'clock. Jean retreated upstairs to her room. Paula was allowed to watch television due to the special nature of the day. Since Connie's father had fallen into a nap in his chair, Paula had to keep the volume low, and all afternoon and into the evening the house was filled with a low hum punctuated by the boings and pops of cartoons. Connie searched for things to occupy her. The house had not so much changed over the years as accrued, the surfaces becoming covered with more and more layers like barnacles. Books sat on top of books, bills on top of bills. Sometimes on a Saturday, or during the long summer months, her mother would have a burst of energy and decide to organize a closet or their tax files, but she usually stopped these activities midway through. A row of worn shoes would stand near the front door for many months, waiting to be taken to Goodwill, or stacks of papers would occupy one side of the dining room table, forcing the family to eat their meals crowded together at the opposite end. Connie decided that her bassoon would be too loud, so she sat at the piano and played a few songs she had memorized. Then she opened up the piano bench and pulled out old sheet music whose pages were brittle and chipped. Underneath the music for "Oranges and Lemons" lay a kindergarten drawing she'd made of a skeleton. She felt the same kind of wonder an archaeologist might experience uncovering a thousand-year-old cup, awed by the evidence of life so fully lived, and then forgotten. She put the picture back where she'd found it so that it wouldn't get lost or disappear.

"I'm going outside," she said.

"It's cold out there, Con," her father said. He had woken and was idly watching the television with Paula.

"I just want to look around."

"You're going to freeze yourself to death," her mother said. She was lying on the couch, a pillow on her stomach, her glass and a book balanced on top of it.

Connie waited for someone to tell her she was not allowed to leave the house, but when no one did, she put on her coat and wrapped a scarf around her face.

She walked across the street and climbed down the embankment toward the river. Ice had gathered at the edges of the water but it was thin and it broke easily when Connie touched the surface with the toe of her boot. The water moved in the direction of the current. Little white sailboats glided along where snow had adhered to a gathering of sticks and leaves. The wind was strong and it found its way into every small crevice of Connie's body that was not fully covered—the triangle at her neck where her zipper left off and her scarf began, the bands of skin between her mittens and the cuffs of her jacket. The cold felt like small arrows piercing her and she knew that she should go inside but she didn't want to just yet. She slipped off a mitten and held her bare hand out and watched the snow accumulate on it. Then she ate the snow, biting down so that it hardened between her back teeth before it turned to water. The air smelled sharp and empty and she took it into her lungs until it stung.

The doorbell rang after midnight. Connie was in her bed but not asleep. She was dressed in the next day's school clothes—a habit she'd adopted that made things easier in the morning.

She left her room and stood at the top of the stairs. Paula had fallen asleep on the couch, her head in her mother's lap.

"Don't open it, Claude," her mother said as her father went to the door. "It could be anybody. A tramp or anybody. In this weather, too."

"Who's there?" her father called through the door. The muffled sound of a voice came across. "Who? I can't hear you." He was speaking too loudly and Paula woke up with a moan.

Connie's father opened the door. A man in a red ski parka stood in the doorway holding a small child in his arms. A woman and two other children were crowded behind him.

"We've gotten stuck. The car stalled out," the man said. He wore a skier's headband around his ears. His hair stuck up on his head like grass. "We were wondering if we could use your phone."

"You won't get help in this weather," Connie's father said. "They won't send out any tow trucks tonight."

"If you wouldn't mind, we'd just like to try."

"Let them in, Claude, for God's sake," Connie's mother said. She slid out from under Paula and stood up. Her shirt was only halfway tucked into her skirt.

"So sorry to disturb you," the woman said, when she came inside. "We couldn't get any service on our cell. Oh no," she said, when she saw Paula sitting up on the couch. "We've woken your daughter." Her voice faltered as she said this, as if she was suddenly uncertain about Paula being on the living-room couch at that hour. She looked up to see Connie, fully dressed, at the bottom of the stairs. She glanced around the room and at Connie's parents, and her expression shifted to make way for some new understanding.

The man put the little girl down. She was younger than Paula, maybe four or five. She stared into the room, stunned by exhaustion. The other children were girls as well, older than the little one, but not as old as Connie. Maybe they were nine and eleven, Connie thought. They had blond hair that showed below their hats. All three girls wore ski parkas and matching ski pants. They each had a different-colored hat topped with a tassel. Connie imagined the tassels flying in the wind as the girls skied down the mountain. Their ski lift tickets were attached to the zippers of their jackets like price tags.

"The phone? Could I?" the man said.

Connie's mother reached for the phone but it wasn't sitting in the cradle where it usually was. She turned this way and that, her hands on her hips. "Girls," she said, coquettishly. "Always jabbering away to one boyfriend or another." Connie felt ashamed of her mother's lie. Her mother finally located the phone beneath the couch cushions and handed it to the man.

"We don't charge for sitting," Connie's mother said to the wife.

The woman smiled uncomfortably. "All right. Thank you. Girls?" The older ones seemed reluctant but she put her hands on their backs and gently prodded them to the couch. The woman looked down before she sat, the way Connie's mother had taught her to do in the movie theater to make sure there was no popcorn or gum on the seat. The smallest girl climbed onto her mother's lap, while the older girls looked around the room, taking in the piles of papers on top of the piano, the old shoes standing in pairs along the wall, the carpet, which was darker in the places where people walked most often. Whisper got up from his dog bed and walked over to smell the new people. One of the girls held out her hand to pet him but her mother stopped her.

"What did we say about strange dogs?" she said.

The man made the call. "How long?" he was saying. "It can't be sooner than that?" He ended his call and spoke to his wife. "I called for a cab to take us to the fire station. I guess people are collecting there. But they don't know how long it will take."

The wife stood, lifting the little girl onto her hip. The other girls stood with her. "Thank you," she said to Connie's mother. "Sorry to disturb you."

"You can't go back out there," Connie's mother said.

"We'll wait in the car," the man said.

"You'll freeze yourselves to death!" Connie remembered her mother saying the same thing earlier that day when Connie wanted to leave the house.

"It's no problem. We'll just run the heater," the man said. "They'll be here in no time."

"For God's sake, you can wait right here," Connie's mother said, too loudly.

"No!" the woman said.

Connie's mother looked at the woman carefully. "Why would you want your girls to wait in a cold car when you can wait in a warm house? That's irrational."

"I guess you're right," the man said.

"Tom?" his wife said.

"How about a drink?" Connie's father offered. "Take the chill off." Before anyone answered him, he walked to the sideboard where the bottles were kept. "You gin drinkers?"

"That sounds good," the man said.

Connie's father made two drinks and gave one to the man

and one to the wife. She held the glass in the air as if she were waiting for someone to take it from her. One of the girls whispered something to her mother. The woman shook her head and told the girl she would have to wait. Connie had the feeling the girl wanted to use the bathroom. Didn't the woman think they had a bathroom?

"I'm cold," the little girl said.

Paula took the old crocheted quilt from the back of her father's chair and tucked it around the girl as if she were a doll.

"That's so nice," the woman said, smiling at Paula the way teachers often smiled at the kids at school who got free breakfasts, as if they wanted to give them so much more than an egg-and-cheese sandwich.

"Looks like we have a party all of the sudden," Connie's mother said. "An impromptu Christmas gathering." She went to refill her glass, and then turned on the CD player. She began to sway a little back and forth to the beat. "It's a strange night," she said. "An upside-down night, isn't it?"

"I guess it is," the man said. "An inside-out night."

"See? Tom gets it. Don't you, Tom?"

Connie's heart shrank as she recognized the timbre of her mother's voice.

"How about a dance? Claude, dance with me," Connie's mother said.

"Not now, honey."

"Well, who needs you?" Connie's mother said. She grabbed Connie by the hands and began to dance with her. At first Connie was embarrassed, but when she saw that the girls on the couch were smiling, she felt suddenly graceful and pretty. She tried to follow along as her mother moved her around the room. Paula got excited and started dancing, waving her arms the way she had learned in the ballet class she'd taken at the YMCA.

"Mom? Dad?" It was Jean, standing on the stairs. She was wearing an old T-shirt and gym shorts that rose high up on her thighs.

"Jean! Come down!" Connie's mother said. She let go of one of Connie's hands and twirled Connie around. Connie got tangled up and she and her mother broke apart. Connie kept twirling and dancing for the girls.

"Stop it, Connie!" Jean said. "Stop it right now!"

Connie stopped dancing. Suddenly, she realized that the girls were not smiling at her but were trying to hide their laughter. Connie felt humiliated. She looked at Jean and widened her eyes, giving Jean their signal that she needed to be saved. But Jean did not come to her rescue. Something in her face shifted and Connie thought she was seeing a much older version of Jean, as if time had jumped ahead and here was Jean, maybe someone's wife, maybe somebody's mother, maybe living somewhere very far away. In that moment, Connie had the idea that she wouldn't know Jean when they were older, that when Jean left the family, she would leave Connie, too, because Connie would remind her of things she didn't want to remember.

The snow stopped sometime during the night. The sky was so bright the next morning that when Connie looked outside the kitchen window her eyes grew teary. She poured out the bowls of cereal. Jean came into the kitchen, carrying the glasses that had been left in the living room, the three empty glasses and the full one. While Connie washed the glasses, Jean packed Paula's lunch.

On the way to school, the girls stopped to watch a tow truck driver working to hook a station wagon to his truck. The high whine of his winch sang out into the brisk morning as the back end of the car tilted up higher and higher. Skis crowded the windows of the station wagon. It had been nearly two in the morning when the taxi finally arrived to take the family to the fire station.

The tow truck maneuvered back and forth until the car broke free of the snowbank. When the truck drove off, the car followed along like an unwilling child. Connie realized that had the car not become stuck, it would have gone off the edge of the road and fallen down the embankment that led toward the river. She remembered how fragile the ice had been the day before. She imagined the car sliding beneath the water and the ski hats—blue, green, and yellow—floating out of the windows and rising to the surface, their tassels wavering atop the water like small flags. She pictured the three girls sitting in the backseat of the submerged car holding hands. They would have been a help to one another, the way sisters can be.

Pond

. . . .

"I'M TOO YOUNG TO HAVE A BABY, THAT'S FOR SURE," MARTHA said, staring at the sphere of her stomach as if it were a sea creature that had crawled up onto the shore and she were witnessing evolution. "I'm just a baby myself."

"You're twenty-four," her mother said. Julia stood in the front courtyard, holding a pair of gardening shears. Already, she could feel her optimistic impulse to get things to bloom in this shady place evaporating. When friends came over (which they did less frequently as the years passed), she'd excuse the skeletal growth of the Japanese maple, or the sparseness of the fire-orange bougainvillea by admitting that she just didn't have the knack. "Brown thumb!" she'd say, gaily, so that her friends could not guess at her desperation.

"Babies having babies," Martha singsonged. She liked to repeat the things she'd heard others say about her, as if these damning banalities were compliments.

Julia looked over at her daughter, who sat in the child's inflatable play pool they had kept all these years along with the dollhouse and the E-Z Bake Oven Martha had not grown out of. Martha's brown hair was wet and fell across her pale, freckled back in spikes. She collected water in a red plastic cup, then tilted the cup over her belly, letting the thin stream plash onto her skin where it split apart into rivulets that ran down the sides of her pregnant dome. Julia noticed the line that started at Martha's navel and disappeared underneath the bottoms of her white bikini. Julia inadvertently touched her own stomach, remembering how marvelous all those changes had been—her breasts growing pornographically heavy, her skin so clear after a lifetime of blemishes, the unnaturally hard shell of her stomach a protective armor within which tiny, unknown Martha swam and flipped.

Martha was no more aware of these changes in herself than she had been of her body when she was three years old and paraded around with her lovely balloon of a belly pushing out against her T-shirt, the lines of her underwear showing recklessly beneath her grass-stained pants. It had been easy for Julia to pretend that Martha was like all the children who wandered playgrounds talking to themselves like inmates in an asylum. But as they grew older, those same children started to make a different kind of sense, began to control their bodies in self-conscious ways. A little girl might hook a lock of hair behind an ear with a kind of dormant sexuality that would make Julia gasp. Most children began to understand how to read more than one expression on a face, how to react to a facetious tone of voice with a volley of their own nascent sarcasm. It was as if they'd crossed an invisible border, but when

Martha approached it, she got smacked in the face, as if she'd walked right into a plate glass window.

Julia heard the door of Burton's Toyota slam shut. She counted to twelve, and then his keys jingled as he shook them, separating the garden gate key from the ones that opened his house, his office at the university, his safety deposit box. Burton carried every key he had ever owned on his chain, ones for padlocks he'd since lost, for offices he no longer occupied. Julia complained that this habit was needlessly space- and time-consuming, but her frustration was underscored by the knowledge that Burton had secrets he did not want to let go of. The lock in the garden gate turned and there he was, his wrinkled sport coat hanging in the crook of one arm, his worn leather briefcase suspended from the opposite shoulder by a fraying strap.

"Daddy!" Martha rose like a whale cresting the surface of the water, seemingly ignorant of her ninth-month ungainliness. She skipped out of the pool and ran to him. Burton dropped his briefcase just in time to take her into his arms. Martha's bikini bottom rode up over a cheek of one buttock and the flesh wobbled excitedly then settled.

"How's my girl?" Burton said.

"I'm happy, Daddy. I'm happy!"

"You're always my happy girl."

He looked over at his wife and smiled. As he aged, the flesh of his face had migrated south so that his jowls formed soft parentheses around his generous mouth. The folds of his eyelids had grown heavier, and his melancholy, forgiving smile warmed Julia each time she saw it, even though there were times she felt his expression worked tactically to his advantage, and that he should not be doling out generosity but asking for it.

Martha turned toward her mother. "Mom! Dad's home!"

"I see that," Julia said. "Looks like Dad needs to change his shirt."

"Why?"

"Because you forgot to dry yourself off before you gave Dad a hug."

Martha brought her hand to her mouth and giggled.

"You have to try to remember that next time," Julia said, picking up the bath towel from the garden chair and holding it out for Martha. Martha walked into the towel and Julia folded the ends around her daughter's girth. Burton's gaze fell on Martha's stomach for a long moment before he looked away. Despite his good cheer, he could not hide his ambivalence. Before the pregnancy, he had urged Julia to let Martha live at the residential home. It was time for Martha to try things on her own, he'd argued, it was time for all of them.

Julia rubbed Martha's back through the towel and Martha pretended to be cold, the way she had done ever since she was small, making a muffled roar through locked teeth to fight off the make-believe chill.

"You're not really cold, are you?" Julia said.

"Nooooo," Martha said in a shivery voice.

"You're just faking."

"Yesssss!"

Julia couldn't help smiling at her daughter's determination to carry on her small, pleasurable deception. She anchored the towel so that it stayed put around Martha's shoulders. "Go change your clothes now, and then I want you to set the table."

Martha took small, mincing steps toward the door off the kitchen. Before the pregnancy, Julia and Burton had bought her a shiny blue kimono decorated with chrysanthemums along with traditional wooden sandals. Until Martha had gotten too clumsy to balance on the shoes, she had worn the outfit around the house nearly every day, pretending to be Japanese.

"And hang up your suit in the bathroom!" Julia called, as Martha disappeared into the cool darkness of the house. "Did you hear me, Martha? Don't just drop it on the floor!"

"She'll do it," Burton said, picking up his briefcase from the ground. The front of his shirt was soaked through and Julia could see his dark nipples.

"No, she won't," Julia said, without rancor. In earlier years, Burton's confidence had caused arguments. How easy it was for him to spend hours teaching classes and talking with colleagues about number theory and then come home and see only the good in Martha's behavior. Julia thought his unwillingness to descend the rabbit hole of her daily disappointments grew out of his relief at not having to contend with another complex mind. Julia was the one who spent every hour of each day with Martha. And even when Martha started school, Julia would often sit in the classroom in order to put the teacher on notice that Julia expected more out of Martha and the teacher should too. There was one year when Martha had a particularly hard time—there was biting and hitting and tears. Julia stood in the schoolyard during every recess and every lunch hour to help monitor Martha's behavior, driving back and forth to the elementary campus four times a day. Julia had spent the last twenty-four years training the world not to treat her daughter like a permanent child, and then to have Burton come in and twirl Martha around as though she were three years old all over again . . .

In Julia's darker moments, she wondered whether Burton's endless supply of optimism was a ruse, a screen he erected that made it impossible for Julia to express what each one knew to be true: that Burton not only found intellectual solace outside of the house, but on more than one occasion had found physical escape as well. She had learned that his cheerful intimacy was a disguise worn by a remote man who waved at his own life as if from a distant shore.

But Julia had become adept at rationalizations. Accommodating her husband did not, finally, seem that far removed from the myriad daily concessions she made. The notion of what it would mean to be a mother was slowly overtaken by what it meant to mother Martha, just as her idea of a husband gave way to the reality of *her* husband. Was she angry or jealous? Insulted or relieved? Had his indiscretions been at her expense or had they somehow become her strength? She knew that whatever love was, it was also the opposite. Her love for her daughter proved that.

She reminded herself of what she sometimes forgot due to the challenges of raising Martha and the recognition of how small her own life had become: that her daughter was all the best words there were, words that people who grew up to become adults seemed to forget. Martha was joy. She was delight. She was glee.

"What's dinner?" Burton said.

"Dinner is a meal."

Burton reacted playfully as if she had zinged an arrow toward his chest. She'd been a bankruptcy lawyer in a downtown law firm before Martha was born, and there were certain housewifely tasks that, even after a quarter of a century, still rankled her.

"It's a meal consisting of chicken and tomatoes and mozzarella," Julia said, relenting.

"Basil?" Burton asked hopefully.

"No basil," Julia said. "We didn't make it to the store."

"Problems?" he said pleasantly, not wanting an answer.

She had argued to sue the adult day program Martha had been enrolled in, but Burton convinced her otherwise. He knew she was right, that had the program not been understaffed, perhaps someone would have noticed that Martha and that young man with Down syndrome were not in the darkened television room watching the science program about termites. Someone might have heard the noises that must surely have emanated from the cleaning closet. And if the caregivers were astute and not simply paid babysitters, they would have noticed the curious change that came over Martha in the weeks following—her silence, the way she sat away from the group, the bouts of confusion as if she did not remember where she was. But was it worth dragging Martha to court? What would be the cost of making her speak about something she might not fully comprehend? Julia had been careful to explain sex when Martha had first gotten her period, had showed her pictures, described things in graphic detail so that Martha would not misunderstand. Then thirteen, Martha's obvious horror and disgust in the face of this information was a comfort and a form of security. But Julia had to admit that as Martha grew older, Julia pretended that her daughter still existed in that state of childish disbelief, and that Martha hadn't begun to have urges and curiosities of her own. Martha's body was more womanly than Julia's, which was slender as a boy's, her breasts mere swells that barely necessitated a bra. Still, Julia persisted in asking if Martha needed to use the bathroom whenever Martha's hand found her crotch.

Burton had quietly raised the idea of abortion. Julia had reacted strongly, as if Burton had recommended killing Martha. Never once had they allowed themselves to indulge in revisionist thinking. What if they had conceived their only child a day, a month later? What if Martha had never been born? Those questions lingered on the outskirts of their marriage like Burton's nameless, faceless lovers: derelict dogs best not fed. Still, Julia's lawyerly inclination nudged at her, and one Saturday afternoon, when Burton and Martha went to the movies, Julia sat in the university law library and studied cases. After four hours, she knew a competent lawyer could argue that Martha was unable to properly care for a child, and that a baby would be an economic and emotional hardship for Julia and Burton, given the care Martha would require until the end of her life. But Julia didn't discuss with Burton what she'd learned. The notion of overriding Martha's agency by demanding an abortion went against everything Julia had ever believed—that their daughter should be treated like a full person even though her intellect had stuttered to a halt. More than that, Julia knew that an abortion would raise the unasked question of whether, had Burton and Julia known what their future would hold, they would have made the same choice.

Julia took to the pregnancy with the earnest attention she'd exhibited while raising Martha. She showed Martha pictures of what was happening inside her, how the baby was growing from a lima bean into an infant. She bought a lifelike baby doll so that Martha could practice holding and diapering.

One afternoon, Burton walked in from work to see Julia holding the doll in her arms while stirring a pot of chili, gently rocking from side to side the way she had when Martha was a baby. She was surprised to see him, and then even more surprised to realize what she was doing with the doll. "Oh! I had no idea!" she said brightly, laughing at herself, but she stopped when she saw his pained expression.

"I like your hair." Burton said now, moving forward to touch Julia's head. She and Martha had gone to the salon that afternoon. Waiting their turns at the washing sinks, Martha had overhead the babies-having-babies comment. Julia held back from reprimanding the gossips, knowing that the owner of the salon had put up with Martha's occasional tantrums over the years, and that this sanctuary of beauty was one of the few places she and Martha could both get what they needed. Julia reached up to touch her hair. Burton's compliment made her feel unexpectedly shy.

"Mommy!" Martha called from deep inside the house.

"What?"

"I peed!"

Burton raised his eyebrows. Julia sighed. "That's good, honey!"

"All over the floor!"

Thirty-two hours later, a baby boy was born.

Gary loved the duck pond. He was only two years old, but Martha knew he loved it just as much as she did. Every Saturday, she would ask her mom to take her and her baby to the pond so they could feed the ducks the leftover ends of bread Martha kept in a plastic grocery bag under the kitchen sink.

Martha's father lived in an apartment near his work now. She and Gary visited him there, but he said the duck pond was too far away so they played at a nearby park or they ordered take-out and watched TV.

Gary pointed and Martha said "Duck! Duck!" and Gary said "Duck!" and Julia clapped her hands.

"Did you hear him, Martha? He has so many words now!"

It was a chilly morning and Martha wore her red sweater that zipped up all the way over her chin. She liked to hide. It was fun to crawl under the covers of her bed when someone was looking for her, or to play with Gary in a tent made of sheets. Gary sat in her lap by the edge of the pond. Her mother sat next to them. Julia had cut her hair very short and went to work every day. She had to make money now that Martha's father didn't live at home anymore. Julia was too old and out of practice to get her law job back. Now she worked in an office and typed up papers that told big ships where to go. Sometimes they had to go to Korea. Sometimes they had to go to China. And sometimes the Chinese ships had to come to America. "That's how we get our toys!" she said, when Martha complained about Yanni, who took care of Martha and Gary while Julia was at work. Sometimes Martha thought that when her mother walked out the door each morning, she just hid in the garden until the end of the day, but when Martha checked, she could never find her mother anywhere.

"You're teaching him to talk. Just keep repeating words," Julia said.

"Okay, Mom," Martha said.

"Mama," Gary said.

"And then point," Julia said. She pointed her finger at Martha. "Mom!" she said.

Martha pointed to Julia. "Mom!" She laughed so loudly that two ducks began to beat their wings on the water. The ruckus made Gary whimper.

Martha leaned away from him. "He's going to cry," she said.

"He's fine. The ducks startled him, that's all."

Martha liked Gary all the time except when he cried. She closed her eyes to keep his voice from going right into the middle of her head.

"Never shut your eyes while you're with Gary," Julia said, reaching out to steady the baby. "And keep your hands on him all the time. You have to watch a baby every second, Martha."

But Gary was still crying and Martha had to cover her ears and start humming.

"Stop that, Martha! You have to listen to what I'm saying. You're the mother."

"Are you mad at me?" Martha said, opening her eyes, her voice wavering.

"I'm not mad at you. I'm just trying to teach you how to take care of Gary."

"You yelled at me."

"I didn't yell."

"Yes you did. You hurt my feelings." Martha started to cry. Gary cried harder, so she cried even louder to drown him out.

Julia reached over and took Gary from Martha's lap and bounced him until he settled down.

"You're mean," Martha said, her tears dissipating.

"I'm not mean," her mother said.

"Yes, you are. And your hair is ugly. I hate it."

Julia touched her hair with one hand. "That's not a very nice thing to say, Martha," she said quietly.

"I'm sorry," Martha said. She leaned over and put her head in her mother's lap right next to Gary's bottom, but sat up immediately. "Gary has a poopy diaper."

Julia put her nose to his bottom. "You're right. Gary needs a new diaper."

"I can do it!" Martha said, reaching for the diaper bag.

Julia laid Gary down on the changing pad. Martha knew Gary would get squirmy if he didn't have something to play with so she got a stick from the ground and gave it to him. "Here, baby. Here's a toy for you," she said.

"Good thinking," Julia said.

"Gary toy," Gary said, and waved the stick above his face.

"You're so smart. What a smart baby!" Martha said. The ladies at the hair salon always said this whenever Martha and her mother brought Gary there.

Martha kneeled down on the ground and started to remove Gary's diaper. Her mother told her she was very good at changing diapers and she liked to do it except when Gary's poop was mushy, which was gross, and except when Gary touched his thing, which was also gross but funny. She held Gary's legs up the way Yanni did with a chicken when she was putting a lemon inside it. She took a wipe and cleaned the crack of Gary's butt. Then she blew on his skin there because this made Gary laugh. He laughed so hard he dropped his stick.

"Tick, tick!" he shrieked.

"Get his stick, Mom," Martha said. "Gary needs his stick."

Julia smiled at her. "You're a good mother, Martha."

"You're a good mother, too."

"Thank you, Martha."

Martha adjusted the new diaper and then pulled Gary up so he was standing. She had chosen Gary's name, and every morning she chose his clothes. While she pulled up his little blue jeans, Julia reached into the plastic bag and took out a heel of bread. She tore off two small pieces and handed one to Martha and one to Gary. Martha held Gary's hand and they walked to the edge of the water. She threw her bread and when it landed, tiny ripples appeared on the pond's surface. Soon, ducks glided over, their green and blue heads glinting in the sun.

"The race is on!" Julia said.

"Go! Go! Go!" Martha said.

"Go! Go!" Gary cried. He heaved his body up and down, his knees bending and straightening as if he were jumping although his feet never left the ground.

One duck pulled ahead of the others. In a violent jerk, it grabbed the piece of bread with its beak.

"You won! You won!" Martha cried out to the victorious duck, which now paddled in a circle.

"No, Duck!" Gary called out. He pointed to the center of the pond where a duck swam all alone. Only it wasn't really swimming. It was still. And its neck and head were not sticking up but were lying on the surface of the water, the way Julia had instructed Martha to do when she was learning to swim the crawl.

Julia came to the edge of the water and put her hand to her forehead in order to block the sun.

"No! Duck!" Gary cried out. "No, no, no!"

Julia crouched down next to Gary. "It's okay, love. The duck is sleeping," she said.

"No, Duck!" Gary said.

"The duck is just tired," Julia said. "He's taking a nap."

"Duck night-night?" Gary said.

"Yes. The duck is going night-night. He's very, very sleepy." She pretended to yawn.

Martha stared at her mother. "That duck is dead."

Julia shook her head to stop Martha from continuing. "The duck is soooo tired," she said to Gary. "He just has to sleep so he can get the energy to play. Just like when Gary takes a nap."

"No! Duck! No!" he cried.

"He's not sleeping. He's dead," Martha said.

"Martha!"

"Ducks die. Old ducks die. Old people die," Martha said. When Martha's grandmother died, Julia cried as she was brushing her teeth and all the toothpaste bubbled up on her lips and ran down her chin. She didn't clean herself. She just kept crying and brushing.

"You don't talk about things like that around a baby, Martha. You'll scare him."

"Why?"

"Because," Julia said. "Because . . ." but she didn't finish what she was saying.

Martha thought her mother looked strange, like the old lady they had met one day at the grocery store who didn't know where she was and couldn't remember her name. Driving home from the store, Julia said that sometimes your whole life got lost. Martha said the lady should go and find her life. But Julia said that it was too late.

"You're not Gary's mommy," Martha said.

"I know. Martha, I know you're his mother. I would never want to—"

Martha looked at Gary. "The duck is dead."

"No!" Gary said, sounding mournful. "No night-night! Nooooo!" Gary started to cry again.

"See what you've done now, Martha?" her mother cried. "See what you've done?"

Martha picked up Gary and carried him toward the parking lot. The car was locked, so she sat Gary on the hood, remembering to hold on to him just as Julia had taught her to do so that he didn't fall off. Finally, Julia arrived, carrying the diaper bag.

"What did you do with the bread?" Martha asked, lifting Gary into her arms.

"I gave it to the ducks, Martha."

"Those ducks are going to get fat."

Gary squirmed in Martha's arms and reached for Julia.

"I'm tired. I want to go home," Martha said, as her mother took Gary from her.

"Me too," her mother said.

They rode in silence for a long time. Gary slept in his car seat. Martha sat next to him, holding his warm, sticky hand.

"Check this out, Grandpa!"

Burton squinted into the sun. Gary stood a few paces ahead of him at the edge of the river, skimming stones. He was nine and had grown soft over the last year, flesh covering the bones that used to show through his skin at his ribs and knees. Gary's scapulas used to stick out in a way that made

Burton aware of the elegiac beauty of the human who was his grandson. This was his curse, he now understood, to see things at a distance, to appreciate—that awful word. His intellect was always there, mediating his experience, narrating his life as if he wouldn't understand it otherwise.

"Seven!" Gary cried out, after watching the successively smaller hops his stone made as it skipped across the river's surface.

"I counted five, my friend."

"You counted wrong, Mr. Math Professor!" Gary said, grinning mischievously, his eyes shutting to slits, his mouth bending up into a cartoon version of a smile. It hurt Burton to feel for the boy as he did, as if the emotion of simply loving Gary included the darker, more complicated kinds of love he had for Martha, who played in the shallows nearby, kicking up water with her feet, and for Julia, whom he had left.

They'd come to this river for the first time when Gary was a newborn. It seemed like a good idea to get away from the city during the heat of the summer, to treat themselves to a vacation after the drama of the birth. Martha's screams had shocked him. Her pain was so different from his memory of Julia's, which had been mitigated by the knowledge of what would follow, the gift that would be placed into her arms. Martha was terrified and begged Julia and Burton to stop what was happening to her. They held her hands and smoothed her brow, as they did when she woke from a nightmare.

That first vacation had been a disappointment. The cabin had no electricity, and when Gary slept, Burton, Julia, and Martha sat in the dark in silence, each on a narrow camp bed. Walking in the woods or relaxing by the water made them self-conscious about their new, awkward family. Without the surrounding noise and fuss of their daily lives—his job, Julia's caretaking duties—their family was simply an anomaly. The roles were out of order—Martha was mother and child, but not really a mother at all. Julia was more mother to the baby than grandmother. His own sense of himself as father or grandfather felt confusing, and he was unsure how to behave. They returned to the city two days earlier than planned. A month passed, and then he moved out.

He'd come back to the Sierras a few years later on a camping trip with some friends and he'd driven to the cabin on a whim. He saw it differently this time, as a place where a boy could explore and play games of pirates, where Gary could yell and march and throw rocks onto other rocks. Now this trip had become a yearly event. Burton rented the cabin for a week and he, Martha, and Gary spent each day by this river. Burton found he could look at the water endlessly, at the way its unified stream separated around jutting rocks, then braided back together. If he stared long enough, the water seemed to take on shapes and forms, only to break apart again into the relentless stream of molecules of which it was made. On very hot days the three of them would sit in fat, black inner tubes and ride the current, letting the wind and the water carry them toward the small town two miles away. There, Burton would treat them all to ice creams from the freezer at the general store while he found a local who would agree to give them a lift back to the cabin. Sometimes the three of them went fishing. Martha in particular had endless patience for this activity, and was usually rewarded for it with a decent catch by the end of a long, indolent afternoon in which the only sounds were the insect-like buzz of her line when she cast it, and the silken uptake of the spool when she reeled it in.

There had been few women in the years since Julia. Burton recognized the perversity of this. The compulsions that drove him toward lovers had disappeared once he'd left home. It was not a late-blooming guilt that kept him from seeking out romance and sex. It was only his sense that a certain way of being was part of the past. Taking up with a woman seemed foolish to him, as if he were an adult who still played with Matchbox cars. He could not explain himself more fully, a fact that caused more than one woman to accuse him of being cold. The freedom of being alone was, of course, illusory. He thought about Julia, Martha, and Gary all the time. He missed them and knew he was missing them in the truest sense. He spent every other weekend with Martha and Gary and this one week each August. He had done the calculations: if he lived to be eighty years old, he would spend only a little more than a thousand days with his daughter and grandson. Martha would think that was a big number. Her eyes would grow wide. Only he and Gary would know that a thousand days was less than three years.

At the river's edge, Gary was trying to teach Martha how to skip rocks. He placed a smooth, flat stone in her hand, positioning her fingers around it just as Burton had taught him during past summers.

"Now!" he said.

She threw her arm forward but released the stone too late and it flew cockeyed and landed on the ground some yards to her left. "I'm bad at that game, Gary."

"No you're not. Let's try again."

He found another good stone. This time he held her arm as she threw, instructing her when to release the stone. It sank after hitting the water the first time.

"I don't want to do that anymore," Martha said.

"Okay, Mom."

Gary wandered back to Burton and sat down next to him on a log. The two watched Martha as she pulled her sundress over her head and waded into the river. She wore a navy blue one-piece suit that belonged to Julia. The suit was tight on Martha's body, making her seem even more voluptuous than she was.

It had been too difficult for him, watching Julia treat Martha as a proper mother, listening as she painstakingly taught Martha how to feed and diaper the baby, how to hold him correctly, as she encouraged Martha to marvel over developmental milestones, many of which Martha herself had arrived at too late or not at all. Gary's perfection hurt Burton in a physical way. He felt as he did when he watched a theorem unfold seamlessly, the sheer elegance of it almost painful to witness because its presence in the world threw into high relief the incomprehensible mess of his life. When Martha and the baby had come home from the hospital, Burton stared at the infant and could not grasp that this was his grandson, that his blood had contributed to this unblemished thing. And yet there was his wife, swaddling and holding, burping and feeding, reminding him of their life so long ago. When they had brought their own daughter home, Julia had begun to parent instantly and gracefully, as if she'd done it before. She radiated joy. He marveled at the way she held Martha, as if her body had not really been whole until Martha appeared to complete it. And then later, when their situation became clear, Julia's refusal to mourn and her unwillingness to put words to the loss of an idea they had both shared during the months of the pregnancy unmanned him. He discovered a fierce and protective love for his daughter but the second baby made him doubt himself again. How could he take joy in Gary without admitting to the disappointments of the past? He wanted to love Martha. Only Martha. The new baby was like a potential lover, beckoning him, enticing him with the promise of a free and uncomplicated satisfaction.

"You having fun?" Burton said. Gary was tracing a design in the dirt with a stick.

"Yeah."

"Maybe tomorrow we'll rent a couple of kayaks."

"Okay."

"I was thinking we'd grill some hot dogs tonight."

"Sure."

Gary was a compliant boy. He did his homework without being asked and did well in school. His teachers said that he was quiet, but that other children liked him. Burton knew that Gary had no particular friends. He never invited a playmate over to the house. In the last two years, he had become obsessed with basketball, spending endless hours alone throwing the ball in the hoop Burton had affixed to the garage door. Burton encouraged Gary to join the school team but Burton suspected that Gary did not want his mother coming to his games to cheer him on. When Gary was trying to do his homework, Martha would sing loudly or turn on the television. Burton could visualize exactly what part of Martha's brain was compromised and what sorts of reasoning were physiologically impossible for her to accomplish. But he couldn't help feeling that there was an ulterior intention behind her disruptions, and that she meant to distract her son so that he would be no more successful in the world than she. Burton was protective of Gary. He wanted everything for the boy.

"You can say no to hot dogs if you'd rather have something else."

"I like hot dogs," Gary said. "She likes them, too."

"Well, she doesn't like too many different kinds of food. But you know, you could eat other things."

Martha waded into the river, her arms stretched out on either side of her, as if she didn't want to touch the water with her hands.

"Like what? What kind of food?" Gary said.

"Like buffalo burgers. Or frog's legs. Or snails!"

"I don't think I want to eat snails," Gary said, soberly.

"Maybe not. I'm just saying you can eat anything. Just say the word."

"Hot dogs sound good to me."

Burton smiled and put his hand on the boy's head. When Gary was little, he would often slip and call Burton "Dad" instead of "Grandpa." Burton could not deny that when Gary misspoke, he felt a little thrill. He knew how corrupt the fantasy was. How many of his titles were misnomers? Husband? Father? Lover? Had he ever successfully embodied any of these ideas?

Martha was swimming a fair distance from the shore. She turned to face them and raised her hands above her head. "Dad!" she called.

Gary and Burton waved.

"She loves to swim," Burton said. Julia had been scared of Martha's wandering off and falling into one of the neighborhood pools so she had taught Martha to swim early. Martha had become a good swimmer. For a few years, she had even joined a team at the YMCA. Burton had felt superior to the other parents, who were busy coddling their competitive children while his danced and sang by the edge of the pool in her turquoise swim cap.

"Is it cold?" Gary called out.

"Dad?" she repeated, her voice tight and insistent. Her arms went down. Her head disappeared underneath the water.

Gary stood up. "Grandpa," he said.

Burton stood, a dark realization surging through his body. He kicked off his shoes as he ran to the river's edge. He continued to run as he entered the water, but his body slowed as he struggled over the rocks. Martha's head emerged from the water and she moved her hands frantically up and down. He could feel the weight of his soaked pants working against him. When he was far enough from shore that he could no longer touch the bottom, he got caught in the same riptide that held her in its grip. The water moved powerfully downstream and he was trying to cross against it. The current fought him, and every time he tried to take a stroke, he got no closer to her. Martha was plainly terrified, her eyes wide as a rag doll's, her breath coming in short spurts as if her fear had lodged itself in her throat.

"Daddy?"

"I'm coming, baby. I'm almost there!" Burton said, but his own panic was beginning to defeat him. He was quickly becoming exhausted. His arms were too heavy to pull him forward. A vise seemed to have tightened around his lungs. He knew he could drown. He looked back at Gary standing on the shore, his arms held out in front of him, as if the tragedy unfolding was oncoming traffic that he could stop through sheer will. There was so much Burton had not yet told Gary.

About the beauty of numbers, about how easy it was to flee from love, about the disaster of choosing loneliness. Burton knew he could get back to the boy, that the water would not fight him.

"Mommy!" Gary wailed.

The word filled Burton's ears, making an exact and sudden sense. He turned back to Martha just as her head began to sink below the surface of the water. Her arms were not moving anymore; she had given up. And as she disappeared, he realized that he could not live without her either, could not *have* lived without her. He lunged for her. His fingers grazed the cold, rubbery skin of her soft shoulder, and he pulled himself to her, so that they were both trapped in the current. She clung to him. The wind whipped her wet hair into his face so that he could not see anything, could only smell the muddy odor of the river trapped in the strands. He held her under her knees and behind her back while he tried to tread water, just as she had held him long ago in the YMCA pool, shrieking with laughter at the idea that she could carry the weight of her father in her arms.

The tide released them two hundred yards downriver, loosening its hold, the river becoming the weak, rambling plaything they had always known it to be. Together, they crawled through the shallows to the shore. He stood and lifted her to her feet. She leaned into him, panting, her body heavy and formless with exhaustion.

Gary ran toward them, his arms pumping, his legs stretching out to cover as much space as they could. He threw himself into his mother, his arms circling her waist. Martha rested her cheek on the top of his head. "Mommy's here," she said.

Standing alone, Burton began to shiver. His body pitched and bucked so heavily that he had to wrap his arms around himself. But the shaking did not stop. It was as if there were a prisoner inside him, rattling the bars of his cell to protest his innocence, hoping that someone would hear him and agree that he had been unjustly accused.

Night Train to Frankfurt

· · · · · · · · · · · · · ·

THEY WERE GOING TO BOIL DOROTHY'S BLOOD. TAKE IT OUT,
heat it, put it back in. The cancer would be gone. Well, that
wasn't exactly it. The treatment had a more formal-sounding
name, thermosomethingorother, a word that was both trust-
worthy (because you recognized the prefix) and lofty, so that
you didn't really question it, knowing you were too thick
to understand whatever explanation might be given you.
"They're going to boil my blood" is what it came down to, and
this was what Dorothy had told her daughter, Helen, when
she called her from New York. There were statistics, affi-
davits. There was a four-color brochure from the clinic in
Frankfurt, Germany, printed in three languages. As they
waited for the train in the Munich station, Helen studied the
pamphlet's fonts and graphics. A frequent dupe of advertising
herself—how many depilatories and night creams had she
bought over the years, and at what expense?—Helen under-

stood the significance behind the choice of peaceful, healing blue over charged, emotional red, the softening elegance of the italicized quotes from Adèle de Chavigny, a woman from Strasbourg who had not only survived having her blood boiled but had gone on to live a life of graceful transcendence. There were no concrete images of the clinic itself, no pictures of whatever this boiling machine might look like. Helen imagined huge vats like those in a brewery—wide, clear tubes with viscous, viral blood moving sluggishly in one direction, while bright, animated, healthy blood rushed eagerly back toward the patient. On the roof of the brewery, she imagined enormous chimneys expelling the sweet-sour-smelling residue of defeated disease into the air. *Poof, poof,* the smokestacks would go, and all the German townsfolk (yes, in her fantasy they were wearing lederhosen and small peaked caps) would look up, proud to know that, in their town, death had been conquered.

"Fairy stories," Dorothy would have said dismissively, had Helen shared such an idea with her, as she had so often as a child, forever irritating Dorothy with her impractical mind. Helen had been careful not to lob Dorothy's criticism back at her when she'd announced this latest and most ridiculous plan to save her life. But Dorothy's response to her own illness had been perversely uncharacteristic from the start.

Most important, Helen realized, fingering the brochure once they were on the train, their bags stowed away in the racks above them, the pamphlet showed no images of the sick—a choice made, Helen was sure, to deemphasize the questionable science behind the treatment. It would be impossible to look at a photograph of someone as ill as, say, her fifty-seven-year-old mother and think that this faintly medieval idea, one that brought to mind leeches and exorcisms, could succeed where modern medicine had failed, or, in Dorothy's case, where modern medicine had never been given the chance to go. The brochure talked about "renewal" and "refreshment," and read like a promotion for an overly expensive spa, the kind that Helen had read about in fashion and travel magazines.

She let the brochure fall to her lap. Her mother was sleeping, lying on her side across the opposite three seats, her knees pulled up to her chest, her child-size feet peeking out from beneath her maroon down coat. It had been a good idea to splurge on the whole compartment, despite Dorothy's protests about useless expenditure (they had taken the train at Dorothy's insistence, in order to save money) and her usual vague, disapproving intimations that Helen's "new" life in California, the one she had been living for ten years, ever since she'd left the conservatory at twenty-two, was somehow profligate. It did Helen no good to explain that her motley collection of jobs—as a low-level administrative staffer and occasional page turner for the Los Angeles Philharmonic, a piano teacher to private-school children, and an accompanist on the High Holy Days at Temple Beth Hillel—netted barely enough to cover her expenses in the folly of an apartment she'd rented in the Hollywood Hills. This apartment could be accessed only by an elevator tower or by a strenuous hike up a dirt-and-scrub path, and had been featured in a famous movie from the seventies that she could never remember the name of, even when people reminded her of it over and over, exclaiming at her proximity to history as though she were living in a house once occupied by George Washington. The very fact that Helen drove a car, albeit a ten-year-old Nissan, was proof enough to

Dorothy that she had embraced an ideological lack of frugality. The few times that Dorothy had allowed Helen to fly her to Los Angeles, Helen had found herself obscuring things from her mother, like the fact that she had, on a whim, reupholstered her living-room couch, although the original material was fine, and certainly not as threadbare as her mother's valiant collection of chairs and couches, which stood in her New York apartment like the stoic survivors of some rending disaster.

Of course, as a child and even as a teenager, Helen had never noticed the fraying tablecloths or chipped china. She had been comforted by the absolute predictability of her home, by the way *The Painted Bird* continued to occupy exactly the same place on the bookshelf as it had when she'd first discovered it at age eleven and was troubled and thrilled by the grotesque and vaguely sexual cover art. A button placed in an ashtray when she was seven was sure to be there still when she was eight, nine, ten, adapted to its new habitat, and the ashtray itself adapted to its inhabitant, so that it was now "the place where the red button is" rather than anything useful for smokers. It was only as an adult, returning for visits, that she began to feel quietly dismayed by her mother's thrift, as if it indicated something disturbing. Was Dorothy refusing the future? Was this the reason that she had forsworn conventional treatment for her disease? Did she mean to die?

Helen looked around the compartment. She had been right to reserve the entire thing without telling her mother. A first-class sleeper would have been too risky; her mother might not have even boarded the train. Helen had hoped that Dorothy, upon entering the second-class accommodations and finding no other passengers there, would simply assume that they were the recipients of a bit of good luck. But, of course, Dorothy figured things out the minute Helen closed the door behind them. The only reason she consented to this act of economic irresponsibility was that she was too ill to fight back.

The flight from New York had been exhausting. As the hours across the ocean wore on, five-foot-one Dorothy sank farther and farther into her seat, until she resembled a child whose feet waggled impatiently above the broken-crayon- and-mini-pretzel-strewn floor. Helen had noticed the flight attendants casting worried glances at her mother whenever they passed, and she knew that they were quietly wondering if they were going to have a corpse on their hands before they reached Munich. She imagined that there was a protocol for this kind of emergency: surely they would remove the dead body from the sight of the other passengers—perhaps lay her mother on the floor of the galley at the back of the plane, cover her with some of those too thin blankets, or roll her into one of the ingenious storage places airplanes specialized in.

In the low light of the train compartment, Dorothy's face shone. She had grown so thin lately; her skin stretched tautly over her nose and her cheekbones like a sheet on a well-made bed. In the last few months, Helen had become intimate with her mother in a way that made them both uncomfortable. During her increasingly frequent visits to New York, she had bathed Dorothy, helped her to sit on the toilet, pared her thick, yellowing toenails, then stroked them with the bright- red discount-store polish that Dorothy had been faithful to all these years. This breaking down of the customary distance that had existed between mother and daughter for decades made it more difficult for Helen to view her mother as a living thing rather than as a collection of body parts and functions.

But perhaps that was a necessary by-product of giving care; Helen knew that if she allowed herself to look at the larger picture of her mother's demise she would be overwhelmed by thoughts of needs, both met and not, and that she risked succumbing to a childlike terror of being left alone.

When called on to be a page-turner at the Philharmonic, Helen found that if she concentrated on one note, and then the next, instead of letting her mind take in the whole sweep of the piece, she never failed to turn the page at the right time. It was only when she lost sight of the particulars, when she let her mind range backward and forward across the music like a low-flying bird, that she made a mistake. She'd begin by thinking about the specific piece—what choices she might make in the speed of a diminuendo or the attack on a coda. Then she'd get trapped in an eddy of memory about her decision to leave the conservatory, to walk away from the possibility, no matter how far-fetched, of being the person who was now seated at the piano so close to her that she could hear his or her breaths and grunts and soft guttural moans, as if she were standing at an open doorway to a bedroom while the pianist was making love. And then, with her mind hijacked by so many thoughts, she would be a beat too late or too early with the turn, and suffer the annoyed glance of the pianist. She would carry the mistake with her for days.

A week earlier, Helen had told her nominal boyfriend, Nathan, about her mother's decision to go to Germany for the treatment. He had almost rolled his eyes. Helen had been grateful for his blunt skepticism, because it allowed her to take the opposite position with a kind of self-righteousness that she would not otherwise have been able to muster. She proclaimed, if not a belief in, at least a tolerance for this latest of her mother's nonmedical solutions to "the cancer problem." This was how Dorothy referred to her illness, as if it were a tangled political issue that might be written about on the editorial page of her beloved *New York Times,* and then hotly discussed with the butcher or the man at the shoe-repair place when she went out each day on her brisk round of errands.

"She's done her research," Helen told Nathan, who sat at the kitchen table of the hilltop apartment they now shared. "They've had good results."

Nathan did not respond because he was not a foolish man. Six months had passed since Helen had discovered that he was having an affair, and their current détente was built on the understanding that he would never again be able to speak freely. A year before, Nathan would have thrown back statistics of his own; he was in immunology research at Children's Hospital, and had a dedicated disrespect for the alternative medical arts. Over the years, he had listened with slack-jawed disbelief when Helen had explained that her friends Wendy and Terry were forgoing vaccinations for little Mandy and Timmo. "Do you know how many kids die each year from whooping cough?" he had exclaimed in frustration. When Wendy had proudly told him that she'd cured Timmo's conjunctivitis by squeezing her own breast milk into his eye, Nathan had not been able to restrain himself. "Right from your tit?" he'd responded, as if Wendy had exposed Timmo to porn. Helen felt a momentary pleasure as she watched Nathan swallow his criticism of her mother's new gambit; he was no longer sure of himself in their relationship.

She had taken him back because he had apologized,

begged, cried, and apologized again. But in the current atmosphere of their relationship he had no idea what concessions to his character she would continue to make, and what could cause her to send him back down that ancient elevator tower while she tossed his clothing from her balcony to the street below. Could he still organize the papers she left scattered across the table into neat piles set at right angles to one another? Could he still indulge his need to keep the refrigerator clear of any food that was even approaching its use-by date? She had gained the upper hand in the relationship, but her sense of victory was overshadowed by the knowledge that she no longer really had a boyfriend, only a set of misgivings and recriminations decorated as a handsome enough, smart enough, bearded, bespectacled man with delicate hands, shiny from too much washing. The loneliness that had descended on her in the aftermath of the crisis was so palpable that Helen often thought of it as a person. It stood by her side as she washed the dishes, or helped Marina Delgado, her best student, struggle through the *Well-Tempered Clavier* while she half listened, half watched the dust motes hanging in the air, lit by the afternoon light coming through the louvered windows of her apartment. The loneliness followed her, judged her, pointed out which of her irritating habits had finally driven Nathan to do what he had done. She was not sure why she hadn't kicked him out in the end, except that she had begun to look forward to the outsized emotions of his entreaties, the late-night talks, the tears. She knew that the high drama was silly, but it reminded her of the kind of person she had once been—a girl who would weep when her rendition of a Beethoven adagio did not live up to the version that played in her imagination, a girl who would mourn that perfection was too difficult a goal to aim for and too crushing to fall short of.

What Helen had really felt after hearing Dorothy's description of the blood-heating regimen was not skepticism but pity. But she would never have said this aloud, not only because she didn't want to give Nathan the satisfaction but because she knew that it was horrible to have such feelings toward her mother, whom she loved—if that was the right word for the mixture of frustration and gratitude and hatred and tolerance and surprising, intractable, illogical attachment she felt for Dorothy, who was as deeply and inescapably rooted inside Helen as her own fractured heart.

Dr. Halverson, Dorothy's purported oncologist and an old suitor from her City College days, had recently pronounced the disease so far gone that the risks of conventional treatment, if Dorothy were to change her mind, would be more deleterious than the risks of doing nothing.

"You mean my risk of dying is now no better than my risk of dying?" Dorothy replied.

"Dodi." Dr. Halverson sighed, shaking his head at her lack of sentiment, an atavistic admiration dancing around his lips.

Helen had been in the examination room when he broke the news. She could not figure out why Dorothy continued to consult Dr. Halverson, or why he agreed to see her, despite her long-term resistance to his advice. What was the point of all those unfilled prescriptions for lab tests? Why did he continue to let her waste his time? Maybe he, like Helen, was so mystified by Dorothy's aberrant choice of the esoteric over science that he didn't quite believe it, and was waiting for Dorothy to finally break down, reclaim her lifelong set-jawed, unforgiving gaze on life, and start the do-si-do of chemo and radiation. Dorothy, this short, mouthy woman from Bayonne who had marched for women's rights and against Vietnam, her small frame hidden in the crowds while her homemade posters floated in the air above her as though held aloft by a ghost, had never once, in fifty-seven years, shown an interest in anything "alternative," or even philosophical. Helen had been six when her father died. She asked how long it took a person to climb to Heaven. Dorothy took Helen's face in her hands and said, "Not Heaven, honey. That's just a fairy tale." How frustrating it must have been for Dr. Halverson to watch Dorothy placing her faith in Dr. Hsia and his stinking herbs in Chinatown, or in Paul Romero and his needles in Park Slope, or in the water-therapy clinic in D.C. Helen admired the doctor's delicacy. He never belittled Dorothy's choices, and in these past months, when Dorothy had experienced her first truly frightening bouts of pain, he had visited the apartment as often as he could.

His patience stood in sharp contrast to Nathan's disparagement. "It's *her* body," Helen had said to Nathan, in defense of the Germany plan. The word *body* sank to the ground the minute she said it, weighted, as it was, with the idea of *his* body and his desires, which had managed so casually to reject hers. She felt suddenly conscious of her thighs wrapped tightly (too tightly?) in denim, her small breasts bolstered ineffectually by some newfangled underwire bra she'd bought online. She had never had smooth skin—had picked and squeezed it too much as a teenager despite her mother's warnings. Was that it? Did Nathan's other woman have small pores? Nathan shrugged, smiled, then scrolled through five other expressions, trying to find the one that would cause him the least harm.

Helen was humiliated all over again. That was the problem with his transgression, she thought: he had taken so many words away from her. Besides *body,* there was *hope* (the woman's ridiculous name), there was *desert* (one of the places they'd trysted). Whole sentences like "What's on your mind?" became as dangerous as stepping in front of a speeding car.

The train made a stop at a local station. It was dark, and shadowy figures wearing heavy overcoats against the midwinter cold moved on and off the platform. Dorothy's eyes opened. She stared across the compartment, but Helen could tell that Dorothy was not seeing, that she was suspended somewhere between her pill-induced sleep and a fuzzy semi-alertness. It made Helen feel weak to see her mother hovering helplessly in this state. As much as she hated to admit it, Helen counted on her mother's decisiveness, her unwillingness to wander around in the gray areas of emotion. When Helen finished with middling results in too many competitions and took a hard look at where she stood among her musical peers, she made the choice to give up her dream of becoming a concert pianist. Dorothy had said, "That's sensible," as though she'd been waiting patiently for years for Helen to get the answer right. Helen suddenly felt the lie behind all those performances and recitals; she had thought her mother her ally, when in fact Dorothy had been tapping her foot the whole time, waiting for Helen to wise up.

Helen regarded her mother a moment longer. The blue of her eyes was rheumy, indistinct. Her mouth hung open in a way that Helen knew she would hate. A few strands of hair were stuck to her dry lips. Dorothy had imparted several important pieces of advice to Helen in her youth, one of which was "Don't hold your mouth open—it makes you look stupid." Helen was also to wear a bra even in bed, in a war against future droop, and suck her stomach in at all times. Dorothy's advice was a warning about how to avoid a dark, ugly inevitability. So, in reality, it wasn't advice at all, only an admission of Helen's ultimate inefficacy in the face of the Cards You've Been Dealt.

Dorothy's teeth seemed yellower than Helen remembered. But everything about her seemed yellow now, like the pages of an old library book.

"God," Dorothy said, breathlessly, and, for a moment, Helen wondered if she was having a conversation with that Man she professed not to believe in. But Dorothy's eyes were focused now. She had come to. "Where are we?"

"Nowhere," Helen said, looking out the window. "We just passed a town. You should sleep some more, Mom. We have a ways to go." She regretted this suggestion. Her mother was cunning enough to know when she was not wanted.

"Whenever I sleep, I feel like I'm rehearsing for something," Dorothy said, attempting to sit up. Helen helped Dorothy settle against the train seat. Her mother smelled of the tuberose perfume she'd used her whole life, that and the turning odor of the body in decline. Helen wondered when this happened—at what point the body's smells could no longer be masked by deodorants or flowery soaps, at what point they would stop taking no for an answer.

"How do you feel?" Helen asked. She herself had barely recovered from the eight hours on the plane from New York. She felt clammy and bloated from having eaten too many meals in too short a time. She wanted to strip, have a bath, evacuate, start over again.

"I feel like shit, darling," Dorothy said.

"Are you hungry?" Helen asked.

"No."

"You should eat." Helen looked into her purse. "I have a granola bar. And that turkey sandwich from the plane."

"*That* will kill me. What is it, ten hours old?"

"You'll need your strength."

"Let's put away the platitude playbook, sweetheart," Dorothy said. "If there's one thing I know about lately, it's my dear, disastrous body. And if it eats right now it will upchuck all over this lovely compartment you've wasted your money on."

Helen studied the pattern of veins webbed across her mother's cheeks. She thought about La Brea Woman. A model of the dwarfish prehistoric woman was posed in a glass case at a museum on Wilshire. She appeared clad in an animal pelt, her long black hair modestly covering her naked plaster breasts. But, then, through a trick of light and mirrors, her outfit, as well as her skin, fell away, so that you could see her knobby skeleton.

"You make it awfully hard, Mom," Helen said, finally.

"Oh, I'm sorry." Dorothy sighed, her expression genuinely penitent. "But for some reason having cancer gives everyone else the feeling they can order you around. Like you don't know what's good for you now that you've been stupid enough to contract this disease."

"I'm sorry."

"Don't apologize."

"I'm sorry."

"Don't—"

But Helen was smiling, and Dorothy's eyes lit up at the memory. Dorothy had despised Helen's childhood habit of apologizing for everything and everyone around her—which was, in itself, a reaction to her mother's uncomfortable insistence on truthfulness. Once, after months of Helen's complaints about a certain irrational science teacher, Dorothy had walked right up to the woman at an open house—a woman who was half a foot taller than she—and asked her if she was experiencing menopause. Helen had spent much of her youth trying to position herself at a physical and psychological ten-foot remove from her mother.

They were good together this way, teasing each other. When Helen had discovered the affair, she flew to New York. It was a strange impulse to seek out her mother for emotional succor, and Helen was almost frightened when she arrived at the apartment, certain that her mother, never a baker of chocolate chip cookies or a soother of feverish foreheads, would only make her feel worse. She had spent the weekend in an old Lanz nightgown that her mother had saved, standing at the open door of the refrigerator with a hand on her hip, pouting. Dorothy had been a wonder of humor, insisting that they google "Nathan's girl," as she referred to her, and, together, mother and daughter had stared at a picture of the absurdly named doctor with the dumbfounded awe one feels in the presence of a masterpiece. Hope was pretty enough, with a lustrous mane of brown hair and the kind of Jewish looks that had been smoothed out by cross-fertilization or plastic surgery. She was obviously younger than Helen. But before Helen could fall into despondency, Dorothy found fault with the set of the woman's eyes, her thin lips, her ironed hair. She could tell that the woman had a "big tush," despite the fact that the image on the computer screen showed her only from the neck up. Her dissection made Helen laugh and feel defended and full of gratitude.

The dim shapes of small villages appeared against the night sky like phantoms, only to disappear into unarticulated darkness. An occasional bright constellation spread across the land, signaling a town of more significance. If she squinted, Helen could make out church steeples, the dark spill of homes on a hillside, and large, low factory buildings. She could have been anywhere in the world. She had never been to Germany before, and now she was seeing the country only as geographic semaphore.

"I need to pee," Dorothy said.

Helen stood up immediately, relieved to be necessary. She helped her mother out of their compartment, and they awkwardly negotiated the narrow corridor. Helen held on to her mother as she opened the bathroom door, careful to steady her as the train lurched from side to side. Dorothy was as light and fragile as papier-mâché. Helen closed the bathroom door behind them, reached past her mother, and flipped up the metal toilet lid, then loosened her mother's slacks and eased them down her hips. Dorothy had always been private about her body; Helen could not remember ever having seen her naked before the disease had turned her into a reluctant exhibitionist.

"I think I can take it from here," Dorothy said.

Helen stepped back into the corridor and shut the door.

She leaned against the cold window, trying to get the image of her mother's thighs out of her mind, the way the folds of skin sloped gently toward her pubic area like small waves rippling onto a barren shore. Five minutes later, Dorothy came out of the bathroom, exhausted by the effort. The door swung shut behind her and she leaned against it as she zipped and buttoned her slacks. Embarrassed, Helen tried to shield Dorothy from the view of the few strangers who lingered farther down the corridor. Her discomfort soon gave way to sadness, as she realized the degree to which the disease had stripped her mother of the identity that had gotten her through so much in her life, and with such grace.

"It's like a prison camp in there," Dorothy said. "You'd think they'd make it a little bigger just to avoid the innuendo."

Helen moved to help her.

"I'm fine," Dorothy said, reaching to either side of the corridor and making her way back to their compartment.

Helen realized that her arms were still extended toward her mother, as if she could somehow conduct Dorothy to a safe landing. She felt ridiculous. Her mother had eschewed help all her life, had put herself through City College by working night shifts as a secretary. After she married Helen's father, she'd helped him open his dental practice, running his office, sometimes masquerading as his assistant when he could afford only a part-time girl. He'd died just when his practice had grown large enough to be worth selling, and even then, despite the reasonable income from the sale, Dorothy had continued to work as the office manager for the new dentist, never for a minute giving in to any maudlin emotion about another man's filling her departed husband's white soft-soled shoes. She never thought to remarry. "I did that already," she said simply when Helen raised the subject, as if marriage were a step in a recipe that you would not want to repeat.

"Would you like me to read to you?" Helen asked, once they were back in their seats.

"What have you got?"

Helen dug eagerly into her bag. "*Vogue. People.* Neruda."

Dorothy smirked. "That's cheap, sweetheart."

"You love Neruda."

"Are we searching for my epitaph?" Dorothy said.

"That's unfair," Helen said, with a requisite amount of hurt in her tone. The truth was that she *had* thought about what to read at her mother's funeral and had made the private decision that it would be Neruda. Though Dorothy was not a fan of poetry and its vagaries in general, Neruda was the one poet she had gone out of her way to read. But was this why Helen had grabbed the book from the shelf on her way out the door in L.A.? Was she this fumbling, this obvious? She began to put the book away.

"Read it," Dorothy said.

"No, it's all right."

"I want to hear it."

"We'll read something else," she said, pulling out the *Vogue* and reading from the cover. " 'The New Stripes.' "

"Read the Neruda," Dorothy said flatly.

Helen checked her mother's face to see on which side of sarcasm she had taken up residence. Dorothy smiled enigmatically; it was the same inscrutable expression Helen remembered from her youth, from, for instance, the day she'd smoked marijuana in the apartment while her mother was at work and then tried to cover it up with some ineffective incense. Dorothy had smiled then, too, saying nothing. But when Helen woke up the next morning she found a note taped to the bathroom mirror. "Smart people are not necessarily decent," it said, and Helen felt as though her mother had reached inside her body and squeezed her heart.

She opened the book and began to read:

Tonight I can write the saddest lines.

Write, for example, "The night is starry
    and the stars are blue and shiver in the distance."

The night wind revolves in the sky and sings.

Tonight I can write the saddest lines.
I loved her, and sometimes she loved me too.

Through nights like this one I held her in my arms.
I kissed her again and again under the endless sky.

She stopped.

"Mmm. Go on," Dorothy said. Her eyes were closed.

"I'm tired," Helen said.

Dorothy opened her eyes and studied her daughter. Helen looked down at the book. Her tears made the words into a bleary confusion of black smudges. "Oh, shit," she said, trying to banish her sadness with ugly words, words that her mother had taught her never to use because they were public admissions that you could not find a more exact, more intelligent way to say what you had to say. "I'm so fucked."

"Or not. As the case may be," Dorothy said.

Helen looked up. "Ew," she said.

Dorothy shrugged, delighted.

"Remember when you hired that Cinderella to come to my birthday party?" Helen said. "I thought she really was Cinderella. *The* Cinderella. Come all the way from, you know, wherever, just for my party. You made her take off her wig at the end to show me that she was just some out-of-work actress."

"I think there is something evil about those parents who carry on about the tooth fairy and then tell stories about how darling their gullible children are. I don't believe in it."

"You have to believe in something," Helen said, distractedly.

Dorothy did not respond.

"What do you believe in, Mom?"

Dorothy eyed her warily. "Is this one of these before-you-go questions?"

"It's just a question. I'd like to know."

Dorothy turned to look out the window. "Well, turns out I'm tired, too," she said, closing her eyes.

The last Philharmonic concert had been a near disaster. The Brazilian pianist on the bill had canceled at the last minute due to illness and a replacement had been called in. The woman, an American, was young, but she had a good résumé, had recorded and performed with major symphonies—all the stuff of a strong career on an upward trajectory. The rehearsals had gone well, and the woman was full of humor with the conductor and the orchestra, and even with Helen, sweetly self-deprecating about her need to have the score in front of her, although she knew the piece by heart and had performed it before. "You'll be my security blanket," she said to Helen, who had been surprised by the intimacy of the remark; she was not usually addressed, except on issues that concerned the performance itself, the pianists explaining their particular taste in the timing of the page-turning, how close or far away they wanted Helen to sit. The piece was one that Helen had studied but never performed, and during rehearsal she felt her fingers moving lightly on her thighs. Studying the music a few nights earlier at the upright in her apartment, she had tried to make her way through it and had been pleased that she could actually make whole passages nearly coherent. Nathan had come out of the bedroom to listen to her and had applauded when she left off in the middle of a movement. She felt suddenly exposed, as though she were appearing naked before him for the first time.

"No, go on," Nathan said.

She shook her head, her face flushing. "It's difficult."

"It sounded great."

She looked at him, trying to suss out his strategy, but his face was filled with genuine surprise and pleasure. She stood up from the piano stool and went to him. He took her in his arms and she stood with him for a minute or two, realizing how refreshing it was to be with a man who did not think of her as a failure the way she imagined so many of the musicians she knew must, the way she tried not to think of herself. Nathan was good that way. He sat in the living room along with the parents and grandparents of her students on recital afternoons, clapping loudly. Afterward, he would dissect each student's performance with her, rejoicing in the children's small victories, wincing sympathetically at the memory of their bumbles. He took her seriously even when she found it hard to do the same.

On the evening of the concert, Helen sat in her chair by the piano, wearing one of her two black concert dresses, subdued and prudish enough not to overshadow the artist; her appearance and movements needed to be so unremarkable as to be practically invisible. This suited her, this negation. It was the only way she could think about herself in relation to music now: as its shadow, its stalker. The pianist adjusted her own deep-red gown, its sleeves netted with rhinestones that would pick up the light and accentuate the hard, swift work of her arms. She pulled up her seat and tossed her loose hair behind her shoulders. Helen always enjoyed the feeling of tense excitement right before a concert began—it was one of the few times in life when you could be sure you were on the verge of pleasure. The pianist made her opening attack with a fury that made Helen's spine shiver. With that flourish, the pianist announced to the conductor and the orchestra that she was going to step things up. She was going to make sure that the audience, disappointed by the program insert, came away grateful for the illness of the replaced performer. She would own the piece so completely that no one would remember that it wasn't rightfully hers.

Ten minutes in, however, something happened, something imperceptible to anyone but Helen and the pianist; it was like a skipped heartbeat. The woman's neck stiffened, and she began to peer at the music where before she had largely ignored it. Helen's breath caught high in her chest. She felt as light-headed as she had when she called Nathan's hotel room at a conference in Austin and heard the voice of a woman in the background, followed by Nathan's sharp "No!"

The pianist's first slip came midway down a page—a B-flat where there should have been an A. She kept going, and Helen was careful not to glance up; she wanted to make it appear that the mistake had passed unnoticed. But she could sense the pianist dissembling, could feel it in the disturbed air between her and the woman. The pianist was trying to muscle her way back into the closed room of her focused mind, but things kept getting worse—a fumbled triad, and then she'd had to turn a quarter rest into an eighth in order to get back on track. When the pianist reached the bottom of the next page, Helen rose into her half stand and leaned in to make her move. She caught the panicked look in the pianist's eyes and knew that the woman was lost, that her concentration had deserted her, and that the strange alchemy by which a musician could be both inside and outside the music at the same time— both aware of the orchestra, and wholly within the space of her own soul—was ruined.

Helen turned the page. The pianist looked at her sharply and Helen knew that she had done wrong. But what could she do? It had been time to turn the page. The music was continuing, the orchestra relentlessly pushing forward. A swift glance at the woman and Helen realized that she was not angry but desperate, and that Helen was now involved in an intimate, silent dialogue with her. Helen gestured with her chin at the music, smiled in what she hoped was an optimistic way. Just go on, she meant to say. The woman had only to find her place in the line of notes and chords, and slip back in, like a girl stepping into the alternating jump ropes in a game of Double

Dutch. She needed to yank her brain away from the accident, the missed notes, as Helen had had to yank hers away from Nathan's guilty silence on the phone from Austin, and from her mother's diagnosis, and move forward, even if there were no directions. But the woman's anxiety only grew, and Helen did something that she knew was patently wrong in the etiquette of her job but was equally necessary: she rose fully off her seat, as she did when helping a faltering student through a recital, reached forward, and put her finger on the correct measure, then sat down, hoping that her move had been just swift and subtle enough not to draw the attention of the audience.

Eventually, the pianist found her equilibrium, and although the rest of the concerto seemed subdued to Helen's ear, there were no more mistakes. The audience was generous; Helen stood by her seat while the conductor and the pianist responded to the loud applause, then followed them offstage, keeping her customary distance behind them. When the pianist and the conductor returned to the stage for a second bow, the pianist shot her a complicated look full of gratitude and sorrow, hatred and shame, all at the same time, and Helen was sent hurtling back to the time when she herself had been unable to make her music perfect, when she had been filled with sadness and rage and hope and the aching sense of being close, but not close enough, to beauty.

Dorothy woke up, moaning.

"Mom?" Helen said, snapping out of her drowsy reverie into full-throttle fear.

Dorothy put her hands on her breastbone. "Hurts," she

said, in a high, strained voice. Helen reached across the aisle to where her mother was now doubled over, her head on her knees. Dorothy let out a muted, inhuman bark.

"Can you breathe like that, Mom? Let me sit you up."

She moved next to her mother and slowly pulled Dorothy's shoulders toward the seat back. Dorothy's face was bloodless.

"Mom?" Helen said. She was terrified and instantly filled with a grief she'd imagined lay in store for her only later, long after this trip was over, long after her mother had died. But now it seemed that the sorrow had always been there, perhaps from the very start, from the moment she was born and first saw this tiny woman who was to be her protector and guide. It had been waiting patiently. She was horrified to find that her mind had made an acrobatic leap forward, that she was already turning the moment into a reminiscence she'd tell of her mother's last night on earth. "We were miles from anywhere," she'd say. "We had a whole compartment to ourselves!"—as if this inexcusable luxury should at least have staved off death.

Dorothy groaned.

"Let me get your purse," Helen said, beginning to rise from the seat. "Do you have any painkillers in there, Mom? Did Dr. Halverson give you something?"

Dorothy reached up and, with surprising strength, pulled Helen down next to her. She whispered something unintelligible.

"What? Mom?" Helen said, leaning close to her mother's face. She could smell Dorothy's sour breath.

"Stop moving," Dorothy said, the words barely audible.

"There's got to be something we can do," Helen said.

"Why?"

Helen realized that she was holding her mother's narrow hand in hers. She couldn't remember the last time she had held her mother's hand. She turned it over, and gently began to stroke her mother's wrinkled palm in circles. "Is that good?" Helen said. "Does that help?"

"Does it?" Dorothy said softly.

Helen wondered if Dorothy was confused. Perhaps the cancer was affecting her brain. She searched her face, but could see nothing more than the mask that Dorothy had donned to barricade herself against the pain.

"It's too much, Mom. It's just too much," Helen said.

"No," Dorothy whispered, her voice barely audible above the sound of the train. "It's just enough."

The clinic was on the outskirts of town, and it took nearly forty-five minutes to get there by cab. The ride was more horrific than any part of the journey up to that point. Even though Dorothy had agreed to take the pain medication that Dr. Halverson had given her, simply getting her up from her train seat took Helen nearly ten minutes. Helen flagged a porter through the open window, and the young man helped her, both with the bags and with the awkward attempt to move Dorothy out of the compartment, through the corridor, down the three metal steps, and onto the platform. Helen could tell that her mother was making every effort to hide her distress, but even with her mouth set and her eyes nearly closed, her expression was stricken. Helen apologized for the jolts to her mother's body, for the cold smack of air that greeted them on the platform, for the distance they had to cross to reach the cab stand, until she realized that what she really meant to apolo-

gize for was the fact that no amount of flinty-eyed pragma-
tism would help Dorothy through this moment. The fact of
simply being was sometimes an unbearable mess and what
was hoped for in life was so rarely reached. The shortfall between those two things was so much more fumbling and base
than anything Helen could ever have imagined.

Helen held her mother as the cab bumped and buckled
over the streets of Frankfurt. She wanted to yell at the driver,
to try to make him understand that he had to slow down because her mother was dying of cancer, but she knew that her
mother's pain was so deep and pervasive that a gentler cab ride
would do nothing to ameliorate it.

The cab pulled up to the curb in front of the clinic. Helen
looked out her window. The building was far from the brewery of her fantasy. It was a genteel-looking Beaux-Arts struc-
ture squeezed between a pizzeria and a bookshop. There was
nothing to indicate that anything medical went on inside it at
all, no symbol of a rod and twisted serpent, not even a wheel-
chair ramp. Anything could have been taking place behind
those beveled-glass doors—lawyers spinning cases, lovers
making arguments of their own. Helen suddenly longed to
stay in the cab, to ask the driver to carry on, take them anywhere, nowhere, as long as she could stay sitting like this, with
her mother nestled safely in her arms. The driver turned and
looked at the women expectantly.

"Are we there?" Dorothy's voice was raw.

"Yes. This is it."

"What are we waiting for?"

Helen paid the driver. He got out of the car to retrieve the
bags from the trunk while Helen gingerly helped her mother
onto the sidewalk.

"My God, it's cold!" Helen said, zipping Dorothy's coat up to her neck, and then tugging her own around her as the cab pulled away from the curb. "You couldn't have chosen a better season for this?" she teased. "I hear spring in Germany is lovely." But she was stopped short by Dorothy's expression. She looked overwhelmed, as though she were facing not a four-story town house but Mt. Everest, the task looming high and impossible before her. Helen realized that Dorothy had not made her baffling medical choices because she wanted to die any more than she chose to live among her withering possessions because she did not desire a future. Dorothy wanted to live. But standing here on this foreign street, she had momentarily lost her way. The path through this complicated piece of life, which must have seemed so clear to Dorothy just a few days ago, was now as inscrutable as a piece of music could be when first confronted—a wild and alien language of signs that seemed like the ravings of some madman until you put your hands on the keys and played one note, then the next, then the next. Helen saw in Dorothy's eyes the same panic she'd seen on the face of the pianist who had been marooned in a sea of sound that suddenly made no sense.

"This is it, Mom," Helen said. "This is the place. We just have to walk a few more steps and then we'll be there." But just as she was about to put her arm around her mother, Dorothy drew herself up, somehow guided back to herself by her daughter's confidence, and started forward on her own.

In the New World

· · · · · · · · · · · · · ·

TOMASZ STOOD FIFTEEN FEET DEEP INSIDE A NEWLY DUG SHAFT. He smelled the wet, sweet musk of the earth around him, felt the close darkness as a kind of comfort. When he was a child, he had been terrified by the idea of being buried, and he had cried passionately at his grandmother's funeral at Powazki Cemetery until his father had hissed, *Cicho!* and told him that he was making a spectacle of himself. But now Tomasz saw that the inside of the earth was like the underwater world, a comforting place, where time was stretched and slowed, and sound pressed in like puppies against their mother's belly. He realized that he would die in America. It was an idea so obvious he had not bothered to think it before.

"Ready, boss?" It was Gustavo, calling down the shaft. In the five years he'd been in the States, Tomasz had built up a small construction company and Gustavo was his most steadfast employee. Often the two worked alongside each other on jobs where the profits would be eaten up by more laborers. Gustavo was usually teasing and jocular, a showman bent on getting a laugh out of Tomasz at any cost. But his tone was gentle as he spoke to his employer from above. When the two men had met at the site that morning, Tomasz admitted that he had hit his son the night before. The boy had a black eye and a fractured arm. Gustavo, twenty-three and a new father, had grimaced slightly at the news but had said nothing, sensitive to Tomasz's remorse. Still, Tomasz could tell by his expression that the younger man could not imagine taking a hand to his child, that he did not see himself as that sort of man.

Tomasz shoveled dirt into the bucket. "Okay," he called out. Gustavo pulled the rope and the pail rose unsteadily, banging against the sides of the shaft, sending a soft rain onto Tomasz's head. Sweating, Tomasz leaned on his shovel and waited for Gustavo to lower the empty pail, and then he began to dig again.

"How much longer, do you think?" It was the wife standing at the lip of the hole and calling down to him. The sun was behind her and Tomasz could not see her face, only the outline of her body, the way her legs were planted a half foot apart, the better to balance the weight of her heavy pregnancy. The small figure by her side was her daughter. As he looked up, shielding his eyes from the sun, Tomasz imagined that the wife's face bore the carefully polite expression women all over the city offered when he showed up to build their fourth bathrooms or convert their garages into exercise gyms. In their excessive graciousness he smelled their fear. He had done well in this country in a very short time, well enough that he and Eliana had been able to put a down payment on a small home.

Their son had become practically American. Teo refused to speak Polish, and had managed to shed his accent. The ends of his sentences rose up uncertainly in the fashion of American teenagers, as if he wanted to shirk responsibility for his thoughts. But despite his success, Tomasz knew he appeared suspect to his employers. He spoke English poorly and with a heavy accent. He broke the language as if it were a stick over his knee.

"I just . . ." the woman said in an apologetic, childlike voice, "my husband is anxious."

Tomasz had met the husband, once when he came to see about the job, and again when he came to collect the up-front money he required before beginning work. The man had a shaven head and affected a confidential manner meant to erase the distinction between himself and Tomasz. Still he complained about having to pay before work was begun. Tomasz had learned that the richer clients were more unscrupulous. They would claim some mistake, point to where a bathroom tile was not perfectly square, complain about a natural imperfection in a granite countertop, and refuse to pay for the work. Tomasz had no recourse. To take a client to court would be impossibly expensive and would put his reputation at risk.

When Tomasz arrived that first day, he followed the couple through the house. It was a modern home with tall plate glass windows looking out onto a deep canyon. The white rooms were practically bare—a few carefully placed pieces of unwelcoming furniture, a child's toy here and there, a single flower in a vase the shape of a woman's torso sitting on a glass coffee table. African statues with large, protruding phalluses were positioned with their backs to the living room, as if they were taking in the view and peeing at the same time. In the little girl's room, the wife pointed out the disarming cracks in the ceiling, and Tomasz could tell she was unused to adversity, and that a fissure in the plaster suggested a world of lurid possibilities. While Tomasz and her husband conferred, she cleaned hair from a plastic brush as if this little bit of house-keeping would make the greater problems disappear. In the kitchen, the man pointed out where the wall had separated from the floor by almost an inch and a half. Tomasz was quietly alarmed.

"This isn't much," the man said. "A little settling. Natural on a hillside, right?" Tomasz took a coin from his pocket, crouched down, and set it on its edge. He flicked his thumb the way he had learned to do as a boy playing marbles against the schoolyard wall. The couple watched in silence as the quarter picked up speed, making its way down the perceptible incline of the drastic floor. The little girl scampered after the coin and grabbed it. Her father told her not to steal and made a show of instructing her to return the coin to Tomasz, as though it were something Tomasz couldn't do without. To-masz told the couple that their house was pulling away from the foundation and was at risk of sliding down the hill.

The woman's hand floated to her rounded belly. "We're ruined," she said.

"You're being overdramatic," her husband said.

"You have a job," she said to him. "What do I have? I have nothing."

Tomasz did not understand. Even after five years in America, he still struggled with the new language. English words felt awkward in his mouth, and he knew he was never saying precisely what he intended. He spoke well enough to get along, but there were still moments in conversations when someone put together a series of words that seemed to add up to meanings altogether different from what the individual parts suggested. Then he was lost, as if the crumbs laid down in the forest of communication had been devoured by small woodland animals.

"He's . . . we're just curious about the time frame," the wife said now. She had shifted her position so that she was blocking the sun. Now Tomasz could see her face clearly. She was pale skinned, her cheeks soft and flushed. The expression on her face made her look as though she found everything remarkable.

"One week," Tomasz said. "Maybe little bit longer." Her question irritated him. On the rare occasion a job ran over, he paid his workers out of his pocket.

"I'm sorry to bother you," she said. But she did not move from where she was standing. "It's very hot. It must be sweltering down there."

He didn't respond.

"Can I get you something to drink? Some juice? I think we have pink lemonade. That's Alicia's favorite. Anything pink." She laughed awkwardly.

"We are fine," he said.

"I should have asked before. It's this pregnancy. I don't know where my brain is."

He repeated that he and Gustavo were fine. Her nervousness made him self-conscious. He preferred jobs where the clients were not at home during the day. When the men were present they felt a need to confer with Tomasz, as if they wanted to appear involved with the manly work of taking care of their own houses. The women smiled foolishly whenever they caught Tomasz's eye. They pointedly instructed their children to say hello to the workers or they tried out their meager Spanish, unaware that he did not speak that language.

The day grew hotter. Tomasz and Gustavo worked quietly, speaking only to discuss the requirements of the job, which were to fill three thirty-five-foot shafts with concrete and then bolt these pylons to the existing foundation and anchor the house. Tomasz and Gustavo paused occasionally to drink water from Gustavo's bright orange cooler or to empty their bladders into the bushes. At four o'clock, Gustavo drove away in his car, which made a grating sound as its low-slung belly kissed the pavement, and Tomasz set out cautiously for home.

The night before, he and Eliana had been talking in the kitchen. She stood at the sink washing the dinner dishes while he leaned against a wall, a beer in hand. Teo appeared in the doorway.

"You're gonna get a phone call," the boy said.

"Too much skateboarding! Too much computer!" Tomasz said, assuming Teo's grades were slipping again. Tomasz and his wife spoke Polish to one another and to Teo, but the boy insisted on responding in English. "Every time your mother or I have to go to a meeting at your school, we miss work. We lose money. Do you understand that?"

"It's this girl," Teo said. "She's pregnant."

Eliana turned off the water and looked at Teo. "You mean you got this girl pregnant."

"Yeah."

"Oh, my God," she said.

Tomasz felt rage shudder through his body. His head filled with static. He could barely hear himself speak. "You're fourteen years old. How could you get a girl pregnant?"

"You want me to explain it to you?"

"Don't be rude," Eliana said.

"Whatever," Teo said, and Tomasz hit him. Teo lurched backward and then put out his arm to break his fall.

"Well, that solves the problem," Eliana said, as she and Tomasz lifted Teo and helped him into the living room and onto the couch. Polish and English knitted together as she reacted to her husband's violence and tried to pacify her sobbing child. Tomasz held Teo as Eliana fashioned a splint out of cardboard she ripped off the back of a pad of paper, fixing it to his arm with masking tape. She had been a nurse in Poland and now worked in the emergency room at County.

Teo cried deep, uneven heaves, his face splotchy, his mouth making all sorts of shapes, the way it had when he was little and fell down, hurt as much by the fact that the world had betrayed him as by a scraped knee. Tomasz felt as he did in the aftermath of a drunken night or when firing a recalcitrant worker, the surge of self-righteous energy replaced by a sense of his own puniness. Still, he was grateful to have his fingers laced through Teo's dirty hair, to stroke the boy's arm and mutter apologies, to have finally landed on something that connected them.

On the way to the emergency room, Teo sat between his father and mother in the front seat of the truck. Eliana tried to keep his arm steady while holding a plastic bag full of ice to his eye.

"So, you think you love her? This girl? This Amber?" Tomasz said.

"I don't even know her that well," Teo muttered.

"You don't know her?"

"We don't hang out."

Tomasz tried to remember what this meant. He remembered about "hooking up," a phrase which made him think of the carcass of an animal hanging from a beam at his father's butcher shop, but which Eliana had explained meant sex. It was a joke between them at night. He would murmur, "*Chcesz* hook up?" and she would laugh and place her expert hands between his legs. But hanging out? What was this? He could think only of Piotr Danielewski, the idiot boy who had grown up in the house next door. His tongue hung from his open mouth as if it were a wilted flag. Tomasz wished Teo had said he loved the girl or that he couldn't live without her, that if his parents tried to keep them apart, he would run away with her. Tomasz could forgive his son for trying on adult passion like a child playing a game of dress-up. But it was as if the boy wanted to deny his emotions air and water until they dried up and fell off.

Tomasz pulled into the driveway of his house, turned off the engine, and sat in the dark. He and Eliana had not yet spoken about the previous night. By the time they had gotten home from the emergency room it was nearly two in the morning. After putting a drug-woozy Teo into bed, they both fell asleep in their clothes. He could easily imagine what she would say to him now. Her years of working in public hospitals had rendered the world blunt to her. You had a tumor, you cut it out. Your husband beat you, you left him. You didn't fool around with herbal remedies for the cancer and you didn't go home and believe your husband when he said he'd never do it again. She had no patience with justifications and excuses; she was not entirely sure about forgiveness.

Eliana was in the bedroom, taking off her purple scrubs. Tomasz found her nursing outfits unexpectedly sexy. The shapeless shirt and drawstring pants hid the softness that he knew existed behind her expedient and commonsense demeanor. It had been her idea to move to the States after she'd read about the abundance of nursing jobs and the better pay. She was the more pragmatic of the two and she had easily put their life in Poland behind her. Tomasz's memories of home danced around his consciousness like floaters in the eyes, appearing when he least expected them. He had grown up the youngest of ten children, three of whom died in childhood. Tomasz's father was a square, unsmiling man who saw the world as a giant drill might see it: something hard to bore through. When Stefan, the last of the three children, had been buried, Tomasz watched with horror as his father leapt into the hole before the bearers lowered the small casket, as if he thought the drop too great for his child to manage on his own. Eliana was not sentimental about her youth, but Tomasz's own history drew him backward as though it were an unanswered question.

He watched his wife as she pulled the shirt over her head. Her skin puffed out beneath the straps of her bra, and he had an urge to touch those soft packets of flesh, but he knew this would not be welcome.

"How is the boy?" he asked.

"He's sleeping. He stayed home from school."

"Alone?"

"He's fourteen."

"Maybe we shouldn't leave him by himself right now," Tomasz said.

"He was not alone when he fucked that girl," she said. "There are a thousand kids in his school."

Tomasz sat down on the bed. When they were first getting to know one another, he had mistakenly thought her impulsive. Within weeks of their first date, she was ready to move in. She was the first to announce her love, the first to discuss marriage. In fact, what he considered romantic whimsy was practicality. While he wrestled with the ambiguities of attachment, she spied their life in the distance and moved them toward it. Were it not for her, they might not be married, they might not have a child. They would certainly still be living in the dark apartment above a cinema, listening to the muffled soundtracks of films as they ate their small meals and made love. He was grateful to her. But sometimes her ability to see her way through a morass of emotions made him feel cheated out of his own feelings. "You're not angry?" he said.

"At who?"

He knew what she meant.

"When you hit him, you made it a problem between him and you," she said. "You have nothing to do with it."

"He's going to be a father at fourteen? What does he know? He knows nothing. This will ruin his life."

"Death ruins life," she said. "He's alive. He's healthy. Except for the arm."

"Don't joke."

"Okay," she said. She sat down next to him and rested

her chin on his shoulder. "It was a stupid thing to do. It's done. It can't be undone. He will live with it for the rest of his life."

He did not know whether she was referring to Teo's mistake or his, but he did not ask, preferring the relative safety of confusion.

He walked down the hall and gently pushed open the door of Teo's small bedroom. The person sleeping in the narrow bed seemed like an intruder—a dour, silent kid who had come to occupy what was once the sweet and pliant body of his beloved boy. Teo was blond like Eliana but he had inherited Tomasz's heavy dark eyebrows, which made it hard to guess at his happiness. His lips were almost obscenely full, and it was easy to imagine what he would do with them given a girl's willingness. He oozed a stink that advertised the body. If Tomasz studied his son's face closely, it was as if he were examining the grain of fine wood: he could see the rudiments of Teo—the pores and the eruptions that dusted his forehead, the patches of whiskers sprouting unevenly on his chin—and he was able to trick himself into believing he knew his son. But when he stood back and took in the whole of Teo, watched the way he slithered across a room like a snake bent on preserving energy for its survival, he had the impression Teo could be real, or he could be a remarkable imitation.

He woke Teo, and the family sat at the kitchen table for dinner. Eliana cut up Teo's chicken so that he could eat with one hand. It was hard for Tomasz to look at his son, whose cheek and eye were now a watercolor of yellow and purple. Teo ate with his head bent low, scooping up food with metronomic intensity. His T-shirt, emblazoned with an image of a hollow-eyed ghost, stretched across his new muscles. A bit of hair on his chin caught the light. Tomasz had given Teo a pack of razors and offered to show him how to shave, but Teo had not been interested.

After dinner, Tomasz helped Teo take a bath. It had been years since Tomasz had seen his son fully naked and now he was taken aback by Teo's penis, his thick nest of hair, the articulated muscles of his groin. He could imagine his son on top of a girl, his bare ass moving as he reached for some dumb, wordless pleasure. Bathing was awkward. Teo leaned out over the porcelain lip of the tub in order to protect his cast from becoming wet while Tomasz poured cupfuls of water over his hair to drain it of the shampoo and dirt that had collected there. He reached for a washcloth and started to clean Teo's back.

"Don't," Teo said, shrugging off Tomasz's hand.

"You can't reach," Tomasz said.

"Get off me," Teo said. "Please."

Tomasz sat back on his heels. His wet hands made prints on his pant legs.

The night before, Eliana had insisted on driving to County even though there were closer emergency rooms. Tomasz had argued, wanting his son patched up and his mistake erased as soon as possible. But when they arrived, he understood why she had been so adamant. There were uncomfortable questions at the intake, and Eliana made sure Teo was assigned to a specific nurse who was a friend. Eliana described Teo's skateboard accident, and the nurse agreed that a social worker was not necessary.

"About last night," Tomasz said. "You surprised me. That's all." He heard the feebleness of his words. He was hedging his bets, hoping that his apology would make it possible for his son to tell his mother's lie when his friends and teachers asked him what had happened. The fact that he needed his son to protect him filled him with self-loathing. "I shouldn't have hit you," he said. "I'm sorry."

"I don't care."

Tomasz felt his anger stir once again in the face of his son's apathy. "Why don't you care? You should care."

"The water's freezing," Teo said. He started to stand, and Tomasz helped him out of the tub. He handed Teo a towel. He wanted to do something, to dry his son or comb his hair.

"I need to take a piss," Teo said, and Tomasz left the bathroom.

The following week, Tomasz and Gustavo were at the job site, pouring concrete into the mixer. They worked quickly to fill the shafts with cement. The machine was so loud they couldn't hear one another, so they pointed and gestured. It was satisfying to see the holes fill up with something hard and strong, to know that the job was nearly finished and that it had been done well. Later, after all the concrete had been poured and the noisy machine was silenced, Tomasz and Gustavo began shoveling the leftover cement and gravel into piles.

The wife came out of the house. She was wearing flip-flops and stepped carefully through the rubble. "Can I have a minute?" she said.

Tomasz stopped his work.

"I just want to make sure you tidy up," she said. She was tense and could not look him in the eye. He waited for her usual apology, but it did not come. She set her jaw, as if reminding herself not to give into a more habitual emotion.

"Missus?"

"I need you to clean up after yourselves. The garbage." She waved her hand around the property. "People are coming by."

"We are always cleaning every day," Tomasz said. "Is there problem with other days?"

"It's just . . . everything's such a mess." A bolt of pain shot across her eyes and then vanished but she looked weakened. She reached over and ran her hand along the leaf of one of the garden plants. Her finger displaced a layer of dirt, tracing a clean path.

Gustavo turned on the hose and began carefully spraying all the plants, washing away the dust. Tomasz resented the woman. Gustavo was doing a job that would have to be done again. It was a waste of his time.

"And the Coke cans," she said, gesturing to some empties lying by Gustavo's cooler. "It's really . . . you have to throw out your food containers. Your lunch things. Do you understand?"

"Yes, missus," he said. He wondered if this was a prelude to an argument he would have with her husband about money.

"I'd do it myself, but—" She gestured to her girth.

"It's not your job to clean garbage," he said. "I am worker. You pay me. I do my job what way you want me to do it."

Her cheeks flushed and her lips grew slack. "Please, don't yell at me," she whispered. "Please." Her eyes filled.

He took a step toward her, but she moved back, her arms instinctively covering her belly.

"I am an honest man," he said.

"Of course. I didn't mean anything. I just . . ." She looked down at her stomach. She fell silent.

"When the baby come?" he said.

"Four weeks. I'm excited. Well, I'm nervous, really."

"Everything change when the baby come," he said.

She nodded. Her little girl ran into the garden. She began to pick up stray pebbles and put them on the piles Gustavo was making.

"You have children?" she asked.

"A boy."

"How old?"

"Fourteen years."

She widened her eyes appreciatively and smiled. "I can't imagine," she said. She looked at her daughter. Tomasz could tell that she could not picture her little girl at fourteen, that the future was unimaginable.

He drove with the windows down so that the wind and the sound of the freeway would obliterate his thoughts. The sun was dropping in the sky and the air was cool on his face. It took him a moment to hear the ring of his cell phone. It was Eliana, calling from the hospital. He could hear sharp laughter in the background. She was probably in the break room.

"She's having an abortion," she said.

Tomasz felt something sink inside him. He hadn't even thought about the baby, or about what would happen next.

"They don't have the money," Eliana said. "I told them we'd pay for half."

"Okay."

They were silent for a long while, listening to the cellular emptiness. He wished he could hear her breathe. She was always the first one to say good-bye on a phone call once the subject of the conversation was finished. But she did not hang up.

"Tomasz," she said, finally, her voice uncharacteristically fragile and uncertain. "We're too young to be grandparents. Right?"

Tomasz's father never spoke of his lost children, but Tomasz's mother spoke of Stefan, Julietta, and Oscar often, and sometimes Tomasz had the impression that she did not think about them as being dead, only as being elsewhere. As the years went by, Tomasz lost any memory he had of these siblings. He would look at their framed pictures, which were hung on the walls among the pictures of all the other children. There were pictures of Tomasz and his living siblings as babies, toddlers, young boys and girls, graduates. But the three other children remained fixed in the single pictures that represented them at the age they were when they died. They seemed to Tomasz like characters out of a story, two mischievous boys and a girl who had fallen down a hole in the ground and landed in a strange world.

Tomasz stopped at a bar down the street from his house. He ordered a whisky, his father's drink, thinking of the man who had been old ever since Tomasz had known him. Tomasz held his drink with one hand and stared at the other, the hand he had used to strike his son. He could still make out a thin, nearly transparent scar on the palm from when he was eight years old and had cut his hand on a playground slide, a rough cuticle of metal slicing open the skin. Tomasz's father rushed over to the park in his stained butcher's apron. He picked Tomasz up in his arms and carried him the four blocks to the clinic. Tomasz could smell the cow flesh on his father's clothes, and he worried that his blood and the blood of the dead animals were mixing, and that somehow he would end up with cow's blood coursing through his veins.

The doctor sewed up the wound and bandaged his hand so that it looked like a soldier's stump. When he and his father returned home from the clinic, his mother grew pale and screamed. During the following weeks, she would not let him out of her sight except to attend school. His father complained that she was making Tomasz weak. Sometimes, he would catch his father wincing at him, as if the sight of his son hurt him. When it was time to go back to the clinic to remove the stitches, his father watched the doctor's work with the breath-held anxiety Tomasz sometimes saw in his mother's face when she dropped a pudding from its mold onto a serving plate, hoping that the shape would hold. As the doctor pulled out the final suture, Tomasz's father turned his head away, as if he didn't believe the hand had healed and was anticipating a spurt of blood. Tomasz had often watched his father take a cleaver to a lamb shank or the belly of a pig. He had always thought that his father was not scared of blood.

Tomasz finished his drink and inhaled the vapors from inside the empty glass. His father had lost three children. But in the end, the man was not scared by death. It was the fact that Tomasz had healed that terrified him, that made him mute and unknowable to his youngest son. Each day Tomasz lived was another day he could die. It had never occurred to Tomasz that he could have hurt his father by simply being alive.

A week later the job was complete. The underground columns had been bolted to the foundation. Gustavo and Tomasz covered the areas where the work had been done with layers of dirt. A landscaper would come the next day to put down new grass. A year from now, there would be no sign that the house had undergone such upheaval.

At the end of the day, Tomasz rang the doorbell and the wife appeared. She seemed bigger than she had even a week earlier. She wore a tentlike dress and her hair was pinned up with plastic clips that he imagined belonged to her little girl. She led him into the kitchen, where she wrote out a check for the remaining amount and handed it to him. She seemed at once womanly and childish to him, and he felt awkward taking such a large sum of money from her, as if she were too young to understand exactly what she had gotten herself into.

"You can have party now," Tomasz said. "No one will fall down hill."

"What?" the wife said.

"Friends. They can come by like other day," he said, remembering her words.

"Those were buyers," she said. "But they didn't want the house."

"You sell the house? But it is good house now. I make it safe for you. Up to code."

"My husband and I . . ." she said, her hand cupping her belly, "we're splitting up. You made the house safe for someone else."

Tomasz left the house and went to the bank to deposit the check. It was only eleven in the morning. His next job would not begin for another week. He drove past a complex of movie theaters. Eliana told him watching movies and television would improve his English. But he knew that if he sat in a dark movie theater in the middle of the day he would feel ashamed. He stopped at the market and picked up food and a six-pack of beer. When he returned home, Teo was there.

"Why aren't you in school?" Tomasz said. Teo sat at the kitchen table eating a bowl of cereal.

"I don't feel well."

Tomasz was concerned. He walked over to Teo to check his forehead, but Teo leaned back to avoid his father's hand.

"I'm fine now," Teo said. "I was just tired."

"You can't leave school because you don't want to be there," Tomasz said.

"I don't care about school," Teo said.

"Jesus Christ, Teo," Tomasz said, his voice shaking. "Do you know what is happening to that girl today?"

Teo stared at the box of cereal.

"Say something!" Tomasz yelled at Teo in English.

Teo looked up, startled by the unaccustomed language.

"Speak!"

"I couldn't be at school," Teo said, his voice shaking. "I couldn't sit there and think about it. Okay? I couldn't listen to those teachers going *blah, blah, blah,* talking about, you know, obtuse angles and all this shit. I thought I was going to fucking explode!" He raised his fist and brought it down so hard that milk spilled over the sides of the bowl. He stared at the mess he had created, then he looked up at his father. Tomasz thought about his own father and the dead children who had betrayed him, who had not lived long enough to mask their need for him with rage.

*   *   *

The clinic was filled with women and children and a few men. Kids played on the floor, or watched the fish swimming in the giant tank set into the wall, their small hands pressed flat against the glass. There were no young girls in the waiting room. Tomasz motioned Teo toward two empty chairs. Teo crossed his arms and leaned over his knees, as if he were trying to hide. Tomasz reached for a magazine nearby. It was a kids' magazine full of puzzles. He flipped through it and found a page where you were supposed to locate objects hidden in a dense drawing of a forest. Teo had liked this kind of game when he was younger.

"Someone circled everything already," Tomasz said. "They've ruined it for everyone else."

Teo looked at the magazine. "Everybody does that. It makes it easier," he said, without rancor. His sense of what made a person bad and what made him merely human unmanned Tomasz. His heart split open for his boy who knew so little and so much.

The door that led to the examining rooms opened, and a nurse emerged, followed by a girl and a woman. Amber had skin the color of light caramel. Her long hair was uncombed and fell in tangles down her back. She wore pink shorts, sparkly flat shoes, and a tank top that showed off her bony shoulders and advertised nothing more than her youth. Teo stood. She looked briefly in his direction but nothing in her face showed that she recognized him, or if she did, that it mattered to her that he was there. Her mother signed some papers, and the two left the clinic.

Teo remained standing. He stared at the floor as if he were counting the colored specks in the linoleum. His hands hung uselessly by his sides. His fingernails were lined with dirt. To-masz stood, put a hand lightly on Teo's back, and guided him to the door. Outside, Tomasz unlocked the truck and they slid into their seats.

"It was good you were there," Tomasz said.

"Whatever," Teo said. He wiped his nose with his arm. Mucus got trapped in the short hairs there, and Tomasz reached over to brush it off. Teo was fourteen. He had the be-ginnings of a beard. His body had betrayed him when it told him to lie down with a girl on a cushioned bench press in the abandoned weight room and find his way toward someplace he could not name but only feel when he reached it. One day, Teo might have kids of his own. But one of his children would already be gone, and Teo's heart would be full of fear for the ones who lived.

"Will you start the car? Please? Dad?" Teo's voice was ragged.

Tomasz did as his son asked. Teo reached over, punched the radio on, and turned the tuning knob up and down the dial, looking for some familiar sound to fill the space between them.

Alone With You

. . . .

As she walked along the hard-packed floor of the Sahara, her camel lurching desultorily behind her, Marie thought about the first time she had been called an idiot by her son. It had been his earliest epithet, hurled at her sixteen years earlier in response to her unwillingness to give him a second box of animal cookies. Teddy had been four then, and his eyes grew bright and his mouth slack with wonder and misunderstanding, as if he had fired a toy gun only to find it real and fully loaded. Marie was quick to turn away and not acknowledge the power that this tiny person had over her. She knew that children called one another names all the time, and that Teddy was only trying on the newly acquired language of hurt. And she was sure Teddy didn't really think she was an idiot. How could that be true when he so often asked her what things meant or how things worked, looking up at her with a surrendering, hopeful expression?

A funny thing to remember, she thought. The desert was working on her like the moments before sleep when her mind kaleidoscoped, and loosened fragments arranged and rearranged themselves at random. Bits of life made themselves prominent, the small, insignificant injustices, the moments when, from deep within the crowd and noise of her existence, she recognized her solitude. She let drop her camel's reins, realizing that the animal, a creature of these long aimless walks and monotonous vistas, had no talent for flight.

The trip had been her idea. Teddy, back from college for spring break, winced when she introduced the notion at dinner. She could sense him about to mount his defense, but then he backed off, looking down at his lap, as if chastened. His silence saddened her. Both her husband and son had lived the last twenty months in deference to her situation, something she took no pleasure in. She did not like being the focus of interest, and felt embarrassed that her frailties were so baldly on display. For so long, a wary caution had pervaded the house. She sometimes had the impression that she was the stone in a game of curling, her husband and son rushing ahead to sweep the ice so that she would not stumble and go off course.

Teddy, alarmed by the notion of his parents breaking in on his backpacking trip through Spain and Morocco with his new girlfriend, Elise, could not finally hold back, and Marie was grateful for his irrepressible egotism. He and Elise didn't even know where they were going to be on any given day, Teddy argued, canting his head so that his soft, floppy hair covered his eyes. The feckless gesture had charmed Marie when Teddy was a boy, an attempt to conceal his transparent obfuscations, the small brilliances of childhood that made it possible to magic one hour of television into two. The gesture still warmed her but in a nostalgic way that reminded her that there were all sorts of innocuous deceptions that one came to cherish, especially when they were replaced by more dangerous ones, subterfuges of the mind, for instance, or of familial kindness. Teddy's reedy tenor rose up a half octave, his adolescence making a quick and petulant reappearance. He and Elise had saved only enough money for hostels and sandwiches. Surely his parents weren't going to want to travel like that. "I mean it might be, you know, hard on you, Mom," he said haltingly.

"I'm feeling good for now," Marie said. "And I need an adventure, don't you think? I deserve an adventure." She felt only slightly ashamed to be playing on her family's guilt, but now that she had introduced the idea of a trip, she could not let it go. She needed them to be together in a place foreign enough that they would stand apart from everything around them and she could see them clearly and make her decision.

Edward looked up from his chicken. His long face was scored down each cheek with vertical crevasses, which deepened Marie's impression of him as an outcropping, something obdurate and fixed. His thin lips moved, and Marie felt herself grow eager and alert, as she had during their twenty-three years of marriage whenever she waited for his tersely apportioned expressions. "That seems like a fine idea, if you're up to it, Mimi," he said.

Marie thought how language was the real victim of mental illness. There were no phrases left that were not brokered. It was a fine idea because they should grab this reprieve of her good health before it passed them by. It was a fine idea because they were all in the business of smiling and cheering her on, of pretending that if she cooked a meal and got a manicure, she was well.

*   *   *

Edward had read about the camel trek in a magazine. Marie did not ask which magazine, because this piece of information, like so many of the small, seemingly ineffectual bombs he lobbed onto the field of their marriage reinforced the fact that despite the measurable satisfactions of their life together, she was very much on her own. Each morning, when the front door shut behind her husband and he left for his office downtown, it was as if he disappeared. She could imagine him driving down the streets of their neighborhood, even heading onto the freeway, but the farther away he got, the more generic he became, until she could not hold on to the idea of him. Early on in their dating life, she had woken one morning before Edward and began making breakfast in his bachelor apartment's small kitchen. When she went to throw out the broken eggshells, she was confronted with a copy of *Double D* magazine lying on the top of the trash. On the cover, a model wore nothing but leather shorts, her hands barely covering the boulders of her breasts, the toffee-colored ponds of her areolas peeking out between her splayed fingers. Marie grew warm and experienced a falling sensation as if she had plunged into the dark void of her own absence. She had imagined she knew this man who was so circumscribed in all things—his language and manner, his emotional range. She had foolishly thought she grasped him like an uncomplicated math problem. Gingerly, she glanced at other pages filled with bullet-sized nipples and fully shaven vulvas, before replacing the trash can lid. She wrestled for days with how to confront Edward. When she finally did, in the small voice of a wronged child, he was not chagrined, and it was she who felt disgraced. She convinced herself that the magazine didn't matter. She had fantasies, didn't she? When she and Edward were together in bed, didn't she sometimes think of that attractive British actor with the high cheekbones she'd seen on PBS? She came to realize, though, that in not confronting her new husband she had tacitly agreed to the foundational bargain of their marriage: a privacy would always exist between them, a no-man's-land separating two countries. At first, she suffered in the marriage, unable to speak of so many things she had imagined they would share. But that had been a fantasy, too, hadn't it? As ridiculous as a young girl naming the qualities of her future husband as she plucked daisy petals, believing this collection of superlatives could exist in any single man. She had been that girl. A wisher upon eyelashes, a chanter of aspirational rhymes. *A my name is Alice and my husband's name is . . .*

"I think I'd like to ride a camel," Marie said, pushing her chicken to one side of her plate.

"That'll be a memory for sure," Edward said.

And there it was again: that quicksand of language. Edward colored even as he spoke. For, of course, he was referring to a memory he and his son would hold on to years from now, carefully scraping away the dirt of history, looking for a clue to who they had once been.

"I feel like Lawrence of Arabia!" Edward called from atop his camel. Marie had finally caught up to the group, which included the four travelers; Selim, the guide they had hired in Erfoud for what Edward, after some negotiation, decided was a good price; and Achmed, a boy of fourteen, who walked alongside the caravan, occasionally whispering gentle encouragements into the camels' distended bellies. Elise, from on top of her animal, turned and snapped Edward's picture with her palm-size camera. Hours earlier, when the morning's coolness was suddenly replaced by a stinging heat, Elise had peeled off her outer layers so that she was left wearing only a pink tank top beneath which one could see the penumbra of her black bra. She wore a black-and-white scarf wrapped around her head, and a wild crop of dark curls poked out around the material. Marie wondered if it was wise for Elise to affect this native turban as if it were merely a fashion statement, but the girl was not deferential in any way, not to the alien culture in which she found herself or to the strangers she was traveling with. When Elise met Marie and Edward at the airport in Marrakech, she threw her arms around each of them and offered up her cheek for a kiss. Marie had been unsettled by the rash intimacy. But there was something artless about Elise, her boldness ultimately awkward so that she seemed like an overeager foal finding its legs, and Marie had softened.

Teddy's camel drew up alongside Elise's and he leaned over, kissed her, and said something Marie couldn't make out, but which made Elise swat him coyly. Teddy's body had finally filled out, his neck thick, his back broad. He had become contemplative in a way Marie would never have associated with her mischievous little boy. Marie didn't know if this was a result of her illness or if he had finally turned into the man he was destined to become, a man not unlike his father—circumspect, his emotions meted out carefully, as if there were a shortage. Teddy was both embarrassed and intrigued by Elise's exuberance. Sometimes he seemed to want to shush her, as if she were talking too loudly in a movie theater. Other times, he seemed to revel in being trapped in her squall, his heart tossed this way and that.

"How are you holding up, Mimi?" Edward called to Marie. His smile was wide, his pleasure evident, his desire for only one answer to his question obvious. He had taken to the problem of the camels with the earnest attention he gave to Marie's debilitating anxiety, mastering all the information he could, as if this would provide a bulwark against the unexpected. He peppered Selim with many questions about the proper way to sit, how to make the animal move faster or slower, what camels ate, how much they drank. When he finally mounted the kneeling beast for the first time, it lurched forward and then backward as it heaved to a standing position. Edward was so caught by surprise that he let out a boyish whoop that released a loose-jointed giddiness. "Are you having a good time down there?" he said now, from his perch.

"I'm wonderful," she said. And in fact, it was now true. Walking was an incantatory process. She felt every molecule of her body abuzz with life. She'd only ever felt this way before in the moments of panic that had felled her, when her eyes went blurry and her mind was overwhelmed by the sensation that her existence was a fragile construct held up simply by her faltering ability to believe in it. When the psychiatrist asked her to describe what she experienced, all she could say was that she had lost her idea of who she was. Her sudden disappearance might happen anywhere. She could be sitting in her car stuck in traffic. She might be in her living room reading a newspaper article. She could be in the middle of an innocuous conversation with a neighbor about delphiniums. The last time, it had happened at the grocery store, while she stood at the head of an aisle. There was just so much packed into all those shelves. And the muchness became noise, and she could no longer feel herself in the space of the supermarket. She realized that she had lost confidence in the idea of herself in any sort of place, that her sense of presence had deserted her. She knew she should leave the store, but she couldn't move because she suddenly did not have faith in the simple agency of her body to propel her. And then the thought occurred to her that if she did manage to leave the store, it wouldn't matter because she would bring her disassembled self into the parking lot, where she would face row upon row of cars, their rooftops stunned by the sun, and still, she would not *be* there. This was the single most terrifying moment of her life. In the hospital, they told her that she'd screamed for fifteen minutes until the paramedics were able to calm her down. She had come to understand that identity was a porous thing, an easily felled house of cards. And what Edward could not understand was that despite therapy and medications that brought her back to some reasonable simulacrum of herself, she would never *not* know this.

Camel riding, it turned out, was not very comfortable. Selim had said something about "sitting into" the animal, which Marie had not really understood and was too embarrassed to ask him to repeat, because she didn't want him to think she was making fun of his thick accent. The guide was pleasant and shook everyone's hand when they met him, but after that, he became remote. Edward was put off by the man's diffidence, grumbling about not getting enough for his money, but Marie was relieved to be with someone so frankly uninterested in her. Two hours into their trek, she asked Selim to help her down from her camel. Edward had teased her gently. "People have crossed the entire Sahara on camelback, Mimi," he said, with the prideful voice of a newly minted expert. "You just have to get used to it."

"I'm happy walking," she'd said.

Edward's expression turned wary. She waved her hand, her usual gesture, which was meant to release him from concern.

"This kind of hurts my tits," Elise announced loudly.

"It doesn't do much for the nether regions either," Edward said. He was not normally coarse, but the presence of a girl, as lush and available as a dessert tray, had made him forgetful. Elise possessed the magnetic property of the self-involved, and it was impossible not to crave her attention.

They stopped for lunch by the minimal shade of a dune. Selim and Achmed set up a low table and chairs underneath a small canvas awning held up by poles. After a few minutes, Selim brought Marie a glass of tea.

"Thank you," she said. He was a tall man, and wore a long, hooded robe over his shirt and slacks. "Aren't you hot?"

"It's the opposite. This keeps the cold next to the body," he said, fingering the rough cloth of his outfit. "Your hot tea will cool you down." His eyes wrinkled and his uneven teeth showed as he smiled at the illogic. He was a handsome man; she'd noticed that back in Erfoud. He walked with a sense of bearing, the hooded robe only enhancing the historic effect. "Drink," he said, encouraging her with a sideways movement of his head.

She felt attended to in a way that was different from the obsessive care she'd received during the last year and a half from her husband and her doctors. Their attentions were too forceful, as if they were making up for strategies they knew would ultimately fail. Selim's advice had a take-it-or-leave-it quality, as if he understood what it required to believe something into being true.

She put the glass to her lips. "Much better," she said, although she was still hot. She didn't know why she lied. They were all careful around this man. It was as though they felt they must make excuses for the baldness of the commerce—their money, his display. Her mind lurched from one attitude to the next; she could be fully convinced of the impressions she was having, and then a second later doubt their artifice, see clearly the warped politics of travel, understand her complicity in an agreed-upon set of rules. They had come halfway around the world to have "an experience." And yet, there were moments when she felt more ephemeral than ever, when the gaudiness of this experience-hoarding made her all the more unsure of what it meant to be living. Edward would not want to know about her reckless thoughts, about how unwilling she was to give in to the narrowness of view that her recovery seemed to require. He wanted her well. He wanted her back.

Elise and Teddy began to walk up the nearby dune, hand in hand. Edward watched them, squinting into the sun. Marie could see him struggle as he made the decision not to follow the young people.

"Give them some time to themselves," he muttered, disgruntled by his wisdom. He sat down at the table with Marie, turning his chair so that his view was the open expanse of desert. He put his hands behind his head and leaned back, groaning with the stretch.

"It's really something, isn't it?" he said.

"Yes," she said.

"Puts you in the mind of things."

"What things?"

He did not respond.

"What does it make you think about?" she said.

"Oh," Edward said with a painful sigh. "Just, well, it's a lot of land, isn't it? A lot of . . . emptiness."

"But it's not empty at all. It's full of sand and little hills and valleys. It's a universe, really."

Edward glanced at her warily. She was not allowed flights of fancy. She had shown that she was fully capable of lifting off and floating away. "Nothing lives here, Mimi," he said.

"I don't think that's right. There are trees. Look over there," and she pointed to a clump of wiry bushes. She wanted to make him understand at the same time that she was certain he never would. He was terrified of the kind of flexibility it took to turn a deeply held truth inside out and he became intransigent as a result. But before she could protest further, Elise and Teddy bounded down the dune, their bodies pitched forward so that it looked as though they might fall at any moment. Elise's scarf flew off her head and released the Medusa-like fullness of her hair. Their screams carried to the lunch table.

"Where are you going?" Marie asked, as Edward rose from his chair, stumbling slightly.

"She's lost her thingy, her whatever-you-call-it," he said, pointing vaguely to his head.

"Teddy will get it."

But Edward was already off, passing Teddy and Elise, his long legs seeking purchase in the loose sand. Elise trotted over to him, and then suddenly, she and Edward took off in a race up the dune. Selim and Achmed were carrying platters of food to the table and stopped to watch. Achmed smiled at the flurry of activity, a boy caught up in the promise of movement. Selim looked on impassively and Marie wondered if he disapproved. Elise easily reached the scarf first, snatching it up and waving it in the air in triumph. She ran back down the slope past Edward, who stood, his arms on his hips, his chest heaving as he tried to catch his breath.

"He was a runner in college. The hurdles," Marie said to Selim, feeling suddenly protective of Edward. "I don't know if you have that here."

"We have El Guerrouj," Selim said.

"Excuse me?"

"Our most famous runner. Two gold medals in Athens."

"I'm sorry. I had no idea," Marie said.

"Why would you know our history?" Selim said.

"I'm in your country," Marie said. "I'm interested. I'm sure you know some of our athletes. Michael Jordan. Or . . . or . . ."

"Kobe Bryant!" Achmed piped up.

"Of course we know American athletes," Selim said. "They are famous all over the world."

She wanted to tell him that she was not a regular tourist like all the others, waiting to snap a picture of one or another sight so that she could paste it in a book and show it off to her friends. That was not why she had come to Morocco at all. But how could he know her intentions?

"Those dunes are not as easy as they look," Teddy said, sitting down at the table.

"It could be an Olympic sport," she said, distractedly. The guide and Achmed had moved beyond a stand of bushes, where they began performing their midday prayers, their wandering hum threading through the air.

"What could be an Olympic sport?" Teddy asked.

"Oh, nothing. I don't know what I'm saying."

"Are you okay, Mom?"

"I'm fine. I'm great really. What a wonderful day."

"It's like you're back to your old self."

She smiled in order to hide her disappointment. Edward would say "There you are!" on the days she was feeling good, as if she'd been playing a game of hide-and-seek. She felt the weight of Teddy's eagerness for her to be the mother he could be sure of. Her husband and son shared the stubborn notion that if they jostled her just so, she would rejigger and work right. Elise stood a few feet away, tying her scarf on her head. Her pink shirt rose above her navel, revealing her soft, tanned belly. Marie glanced at the men kneeling on their prayer mats and felt a sudden impatience with the girl. Had she no idea about the manners and customs of the country she was in? And there was Teddy, watching his girlfriend with a dumb, mesmerized expression on his face. How feckless he was. The boy had never prayed a day in his life. She had given him everything she was capable of and yet he knew nothing!

Elise ran to the table and sat down heavily on Teddy's lap. She leaned back against him, closing her eyes and smiling with coital suggestiveness.

Teddy pushed her away from him. "Sorry," he said to his mother, embarrassed.

"I'm not insulted by affection," Marie said. "Or by sex, for that matter."

"Mom!" Teddy said.

"You're not a child, Teddy," Marie said urgently, hoping she was right.

After lunch, Elise was sick. She blamed the food.

"You might have picked up a bug," Marie said. She had agreed to stay behind at the lunch site with Elise while the rest of the party rode ahead to the evening camp. There was some argument about this, with both Teddy and Edward demanding to stay behind as Elise's protectors. But Marie was adamant. She reminded them that she did not intend to ride her camel, and that they would make much faster time without her. By some prearrangement, the camp was being set up in advance of the group's arrival by associates of Selim who had a jeep. Selim would drive back and retrieve the women. Knowledge of the jeep and the fact that they were obviously close to a road or a town made the whole project of the trek exactly what it was—the stuff of tourist fantasy. Marie was tired of the camels, tired of the ersatz colonial charade of teatime in the middle of the desert.

"Have you been drinking the water?" She and Elise sat at the little table underneath the canopy Selim had left standing.

"No," Elise said. "But I remember one bite of chicken that tasted funny. Oh, God."

Without bothering to move from her chair, she leaned over and vomited. Marie reached for the girl's hair to hold it away from the mess.

"Fuck," Elise gasped, as she sat up. She used the back of her hand to wipe her mouth and looked at Marie. "Sorry," she said. "Oh, shit."

Marie dropped the girl's hair. "Would you like some water?"

"Okay." She drank, then handed the bottle back to Marie, like a child handing her mother her used Kleenex. "At least Teddy doesn't have to see this part."

"He's thrown up a few times in his life," Marie said.

"It's not exactly sexy."

Marie thought about Edward's voice coming through the bathroom door: *You okay in there?* Her face against the cool tiles of the floor, the tiny box of a room a kind of calming embrace as she waited for the bottle of sleeping pills to take effect, for darkness to block out the shiny whiteness of the floor, for release. He'd had to break the lock on the door.

"In sickness and in health," Marie said.

Elise's eyes widened. "Whoa! We're not getting married or anything."

"I know that. I was just remembering."

"We've only been going out for a few months. Who knows what will happen. I mean I don't even really know him."

Teddy had shrugged on and off a series of girls throughout high school without much visible turmoil. But Marie had watched him these past few days. His arm slid around Elise's waist or shoulders whenever she was within reach, the way he used to reach for Marie's hand when they would walk on a busy street or through a crowded store, uncertain of his wholeness without her.

"You have lovely hair," Marie said.

Elise touched her curls self-consciously. "I hated it when I was younger. I used to pull on it to get it to lie flat." She shrugged. "It's Jewish hair." She looked at Marie. "Did Teddy tell you I was Jewish?"

"No."

"He told me you never met a Jew until you went to college."

"I grew up in a very small town."

"That's just so crazy," Elise said. "I mean that's how prejudice starts."

"I'm not prejudiced."

"Sometimes people don't think they are, but they are."

"I'm not prejudiced," Marie repeated, irritated by having to defend herself to this girl.

"I'm just talking theoretically. I mean it's worth thinking about, right? Instead of just accepting that most people aren't because we know it's the wrong way to be, maybe we should accept that most people are and start from there."

"But I don't believe that's true."

Elise shrugged. "Look at this thing with Selim."

"What about Selim?"

"He carries our bags. He cooks us meals."

"That's his job. He's making a living."

"We didn't even invite him and Achmed to eat lunch with us."

Marie looked at the girl's breasts, pushing out at her tank top. She reminded Marie of herself as a girl, plucking those ridiculous daisy petals, certain of everything. One day Elise would discover a secret or a lie, a dirty magazine in the trash, and she would have to decide if she could manage all the opposites at once.

Elise stood up and ran behind a low, barren bush. Her body was barely obscured as she retched. Looking clammy, she returned to the table.

"I'm sweating," Elise said.

Marie stood up, concerned. "Let me check your temperature." Without thinking, she put both her hands on each side of the girl's face and brought her mouth to Elise's forehead, her dry lips always the more reliable indicator of fever than her hands.

"You're cool as a cuke," Marie said.

"A what?"

"A cucumber. It's something my mother used to say." She sat down again.

Elise put her own hand to her forehead as if to contradict Marie, but then dropped it and sat. She leaned over and put her head in Marie's lap. "Can I ask you something?

"Yes," Marie said.

"How are you sick?"

Adrenaline flooded Marie's body, leaving her feeling unsteady in her chair.

"I mean, Teddy told me. But I don't really get it."

"What does he say?"

"That you had a breakdown. And that you get depressed. But, I mean, what's it feel like?"

Marie looked at the desert. Maybe Edward was right: it was nothingness. She was nothing in it. She could feel an incipient panic take root.

"I mean, I get bummed out too," Elise said. "But I don't want to kill myself." She sat up and looked at Marie's face. She was not being glib. She was frightened. "Sometimes, when he's asleep and I'm lying next to him, I try to imagine taking my life. Ending it. Saying good-bye. I can't imagine it."

Marie remembered taking Teddy to the sea for the first time, trying to explain to him how far he could go before he would become defeated by the power of the water. He needed to intuit where the invisible line lay that separated safety from danger. The signs were so slight, so easily missed. It was only experience that would teach him. Marie lifted her hand to

Elise's head and ran her fingers through the tangles of the girl's hair. She felt her anxiety ebb.

"It's not something that you imagine," she said. "It's something real."

By the time Selim arrived and drove them to the campsite, the sun had set and the sky was a deep iron blue. Already the sand was recovering from the pummeling heat of the day. Teddy and Edward both rushed to the jeep, each solicitous of the weakened Elise.

"We've made up her bed," Edward said, helping Elise down from the jeep. He reached back and put her arm around his taller shoulder so that she hobbled beside him, as though her foot and not her stomach were the cause of her troubles.

"I've got it, Dad," Teddy said, smoothly taking Elise from his father, so that Edward was left empty-handed.

"Let her rest!" Edward called after them. He watched unhappily as Teddy and Elise disappeared inside their tent. "You're okay, Mimi?" he said. "I was worried about you alone out there."

"I wasn't alone. Elise took good care of me."

Elise laughed from within her tent.

"He should let her be," Edward said to no one in particular.

That night, the stars broke out across the sky, nearly obliterating the blackness. Their quantity was overwhelming. Marie was stunned. The sky was like a woman who had been gifted with a surfeit of brilliant jewels and, unable to choose among them, wore them all at once.

"Kids! Kids!" Edward called, drawing Teddy and Elise from their tent. "You have to see this!"

Elise and Teddy stood, necks craned, silenced by the view. Edward, puffed up as though he himself had produced this wonder, pointed out Cassiopeia.

"I don't see it," Elise said.

"There." Teddy pointed. "See? It's amazing, Dad."

"I don't see it!" Elise whined.

"It's right there," Edward said, still pointing at the sky. "Plain as day."

"Oh, I see it," Elise said, her voice low and thick with pleasure.

Edward stood back, his expression contorting slightly as he watched the young couple discover the sky. Marie remembered when Edward had shown Teddy how to cast a rod, his pride in his own mentoring replaced by the recognition of loss as Teddy easily grasped the technique. Marie understood that for her husband, knowledge was his defense against emptiness. How hard it had been for him, this year, to have understood so little of what she was experiencing. She had betrayed him. She hadn't meant to. But that is what had happened.

Marie chose not to sleep that night. When she'd begun to take the dulling medications, she'd taught herself how to defy sleep. The skill had felt like some measure of victory over her situation. She had loved the nighttime hours especially, when she was not assaulted by the raucous sounds of the day—the car doors opening and slamming shut, the Doppler of the neighborhood children's voices as they walked to and from school. Unmistakable rustlings came from Teddy and Elise's tent, and then stifled moans. Edward turned in his sleeping bag and opened his eyes for a moment. His face was soft, his expression confused.

"Shhhh," she whispered, until his eyelids lowered and his breathing became light again. Carefully, she took his hand in hers. She felt its weight, the warmth of it despite the cold air. She thought of him foolishly chasing after the girl. And why not? Weren't they all turning toward the sun, yearning for life? It was only that they had discovered that they needed to look away from one another to find their futures. She had come to the desert in order to make a decision. She had once been unable to imagine living. But now she could *only* imagine it. Life was a needy child that you wished both to hold and escape from. She could envision herself inside the tumult, the confusion, the utter illogic of it. She believed she could endure the terror. But she could only manage it alone. But she could not pretend to be other than who she was.

She thought about how it could happen. Would she pack her things and drive away while Edward was at work? Or would she stay and confront him with her choice when he returned at the end of the day? A conversation might be difficult for him. It would demand words he did not have, feelings he could not name. She did not want to be unkind. She closed her eyes and saw the stars against the infinite night of her eyelids. She imagined their migration to some other part of the world. Soon, in a place far away, other people would look up and point and wonder and realize that they were only strangers visiting a foreign land.

About the Author

· · · · · · · · · · · · · · ·

Marisa Silver made her fiction debut in *The New Yorker* when she was featured in that magazine's first "Debut Fiction" issue. Her collection of short stories, *Babe in Paradise,* was named a *New York Times* Notable Book of the Year and was a *Los Angeles Times* Best Book of the Year. She is the author of the novels *No Direction Home* and *The God of War,* which was a finalist for the Los Angeles Times Book Prize for fiction. She is the winner of the O. Henry Prize, and her work has been included in *Best American Stories* as well as other anthologies. She lives in Los Angeles with her husband and two sons.

Acknowledgments
· · · · · · · · · · · · · ·

My heartfelt appreciation and gratitude go out to: Sarah Hochman, Julia Prosser, Wendy Sheanin, and the team at Simon & Schuster for their intelligence, dedication, and support; Kimberly Burns for making this entirely too much fun; Henry Dunow for always seeing exactly where I need to go; Deborah Treisman and *The New Yorker* for first publishing many of the stories in this collection; and Ken, Henry, and Oliver to whom much more than thanks is due.

ML   4/D